FLASH POINT

A JOAN KAHN BOOK

Books by Michael Gilbert

Flash Point
The 92nd Tiger
The Body of a Girl
The Family Tomb
Overdrive
Game Without Rules
The Crack in the Teacup
After the Fine Weather
Blood and Judgment
Be Shot for Sixpence
The Country-House Burglar
Fear to Tread
The Danger Within
Death Has Deep Roots
Smallbone Deceased
He Didn't Mind Danger

MICHAEL GILBERT

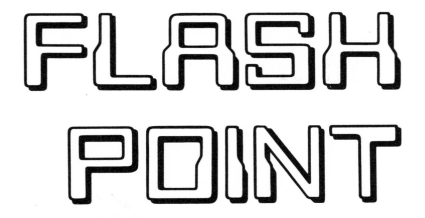

FLASH POINT

HARPER & ROW, PUBLISHERS

NEW YORK,

EVANSTON,

SAN FRANCISCO,

LONDON

A HARPER NOVEL OF LAW AND LAWLESSNESS

406691

FIRST U.S. EDITION

Designed by Sidney Feinberg

Library of Congress Cataloging in Publication Data

Gilbert, Michael Francis, 1912–
  Flash point.
  I. Title.
PZ3.G37367F3 [PR6013.I3335] 823'.9'14 74–5798
ISBN 0–06–011518–1

Author's Note

In a book I wrote some years ago about the law I said, "There is no point in concealing the fact that London solicitors work in certain well-known and well-defined areas; nor would much purpose be served by giving these fictitious names." This did not appear to upset anyone, and I hope that the same tolerance will be extended not only to the lawyers of all branches—solicitors, barristers, magistrates, and judges—who feature in this book, but also to politicians and the press. The mention of the holder of an office has no reference whatever to any particular holder of that office, past or present. All the characters in this novel are entirely imaginary. It should also be noted that both the major political parties have their headquarters in Smith Square, Westminster.

So in all governments there are necessary offices which are not only vile, but vicious too: vices which have there a place, and help to make up the seam in our piecing, as poisons are useful for the preservation of health. If they become excusable, because they are of use to us, and that the common necessity covers their true qualities, we are to resign this part to the most robust and least fearful of the people, who sacrifice their honour and conscience, as others of old sacrificed their lives, for the good of their country, we who are weaker taking upon us the parts that are more easy and less hazardous. The public good requires that men should betray and lie and murder.

Montaigne, *Essays*
(Hazlitt translation)

Laurence Fairbrass was head of the Professional Purposes Section of the Law Society, which is its largest and most important section and employs eight assistant solicitors. He had a red face, crinkly gray hair, and an engaging smile which sometimes made unwary people think he was soft. No one made that mistake twice. He was perched on the corner of Christopher Martingale's desk, swinging one neatly trousered leg.

"*Not* Jonas Killey," said Christopher. "Not *again?*"

"That's right."

"What did he want this time?"

"He said he's got a new angle on that business of his."

"It's got more angles than Euclid."

"You'd better get the papers up."

"I've had them up a dozen times already."

"Make it a baker's dozen. And talking of Killey, did you see Will Dylan on the box last night?"

"No, I was working."

"Good show," said Laurence with a grin. "I like to see my young men keeping their snotty little noses to the grindstone. You missed something though. It was a discussion program. Will Dylan and a trade union official against the managing director of ICI and someone from the London School of Economics."

"It doesn't sound like my sort of program."

"They were all quite good, but Will was out of their class. It was like watching Bradman batting against minor county bowling. He had a way of taking over the other chap's argument when it had got a bit tangled, restating it in clearer terms, and then picking it up and shaking it until most of the fallacies had fallen out."

"All right," said Christopher patiently, "Dylan's a good chap, and Jonas has got his knife with him. We all know that. What are we supposed to do about it? And anyway, why me?"

"You know Jonas. You were in the same firm together."

"We were at Sexton and Lambard together for three years," agreed Christopher. "And I asked him home a couple of times for the weekend. And all the time he was there he talked about nothing but ACAT and MG and ASIA."

"There you are," said Laurence. "You're our local expert on the case. One glance at the papers and you'll have it at your fingertips."

He breezed out happily.

When Christopher had dealt with his mail, he made his way down to Filing. Old Reiss, the head filing clerk, extracted the bulging orange-colored folder which was labeled "Killey vs. ACAT," and Christopher spent the next two hours rereading the papers in it.

Killey versus ACAT. One of the great unfought battles of the world.

It was in 1965 that the Mining and General Metal Workers Union, familiarly known as MG, had swallowed the Aluminium, Copper, and Allied Trades Union, less familiarly known as ACAT, just like the whale swallowing Jonah. As in the Bible, so in this case, Jonah had not been entirely unhappy about it. There was a lot to be said for whales. Big, slow, solid, comfortable creatures. With its five or six hundred members ACAT hadn't packed many punches. MG on the other hand packed a very big punch indeed.

When Christopher first read the papers, it had occurred to him that the marriage might have been consummated a bit hastily. The 1964 Trade Union (Amalgamation) Act had been passed to make mergers easier; but it was a new act, and there were pitfalls in it. It did seem possible that the organizers of the merger had fallen into one of them.

It was a purely technical point.

The rule book of ACAT didn't allow apprentice members to vote on motions. Accordingly, the meetings which had been called to vote on the merger had been confined to full members. What had been overlooked was that the Act laid down that on this question of merger *all* members must be allowed to vote no matter what the rule book might say.

This law produced several of the sort of nice points which lawyers enjoy; and it was clear that Jonas Killey had licked his lips over them. At that time he was a salaried solicitor with Markstein, Paice and Pennington of Sheffield. And he had been given the job, under the senior partner Arnold Markstein, of drafting the instrument of amalgamation and the new rule book. He had done most of this work on his own.

Fortunately, or unfortunately, depending on which way you looked at it, Jonas had been off sick when the actual meetings were held. When he came back, he had studied the records of those meetings and had started to fuss.

In the file there was a memorandum which he had written to his senior partner. It was six pages long and crammed with references to statutory enactments and decided cases. But what must have annoyed Arnold Markstein most was the suggestion underlying every other sentence that if only he, Jonas Killey, had been in charge, things would not have been mishandled in the way they had been.

After this the air grew thick with memoranda. Sections of half a dozen trade union acts were cited. Cases were disinterred from the early years of the reign of Queen Victoria, and that unpredictable fowl Natural Justice hovered in the wings.

When Mr. Markstein had had enough of this, he introduced a rule of his own, which was that junior employees should be seen and not heard. Jonas was notified that his services were no longer required, and he came south to London looking for a job.

One might have thought that this would have been the end of the matter. In nine hundred and ninety-nine cases out of a thousand, thought Christopher, it would have been. But not with Jonas. Jonas came from Lincolnshire where they have a word, "clench."

It means what it sounds like. Rigid. Uncompromising, prickly, with a bit of a grudge against life. That was Jonas in one word.

After coming south, he had approached, in turn, the Registrar of Friendly Societies, the Trade Union Council, his own member of Parliament, the Law Chancellor, and various organs of the national press. Finally he had tried the Law Society. That was where the file had first landed, with a dull thud, on Christopher Martingale's desk.

When he had finished reading it, Christopher stuffed all the papers back into the folder and went along to see Laurence. He said, "All right, I've reread it. So what do you want me to do?"

"You must choke him off. He's getting the law a bad name."

"You won't choke him off easily. It's his life's work. He explained it all to me on two seven-mile walks."

"Then find out what he wants *us* to do. And persuade him that we can't do it."

"I'm not sure," said Christopher, "that it hasn't got beyond the stage of actually doing anything at all. He just *knows* that ACAT broke the rules. I suppose the only thing they could really do would be to have the meetings all over again."

"But it was years ago."

"Time means very little to Jonas."

"It wouldn't be the same members. And the apprentice

4

members who ought to have voted will be full members by now."

"That's right," said Christopher. "And some of the full members who did vote will have retired or died. Of course it's mad. The whole thing's mad."

Laurence took off his glasses and chewed the end of the earpiece for a bit. Then he said, "He must have *some* idea of what he wants."

"I believe that if Will Dylan got up in public and admitted that Jonas was right, he might feel that honor was satisfied."

"Why Dylan in particular?"

"He was secretary and treasurer of ACAT at the time. It was his first union job. He ran the meetings."

Laurence said, "Of course you can hardly judge from seeing someone once on television, but he seemed quite a reasonable sort of cove. Do you think he'd play?"

"He comes from Yorkshire," said Christopher. "Yorkshiremen aren't noted for admitting they're wrong. Look at the trouble they've been having with their cricket team."

He knew this would divert Laurence, who was mad about cricket and still played a good game, although he was over fifty. It was ten minutes before they got back to Jonas. Then Laurence said, "You'll have to go down to see Killey. His office is in Wimbledon. It won't take long."

"Certainly I'll go see him. But what am I meant to do? He's even less likely than Dylan to admit he was wrong. This is his life's work. His one-man crusade."

"He told me on the telephone last night that he's got some new evidence."

"He's flogging a dead horse. Not only a dead horse. One that's been buried and forgotten by everyone but him."

"We're here to serve the profession. He says he wants to talk to us. If you don't go down to see him, he'll come up here and talk to me. And I'm busier than you are."

Christopher couldn't deny this. Laurence said, "I've had another idea. I saw something in the *Watchman* about Dylan the other day."

"That's right. They're doing a profile on him. As a matter of fact it's my brother-in-law who's doing it. Pat Mauger."

"And when they do these profiles, they follow their man round for weeks, don't they. And chat him up. Your brother-in-law must have got to know him pretty well. Do you think he'd help? Slip in a word that we think this thing ought to be decently buried."

"He might."

"Give him lunch and try it out. The Law Society will pay. Any reasonable amount," he added hastily.

"You really mean that?"

Laurence looked at the file, which was four inches thick. He said, "If you can get this bloody man off our neck, it'll be cheap at the price."

Christopher telephoned Jonas after lunch. Jonas said, "Well, well, fancy hearing from you again. I thought now you'd joined the Establishment you wouldn't have time to talk to a poor hard-working practitioner."

This was Jonas in a playful mood.

Christopher said that was exactly what he *was* planning to do. When could he come and see him?

"You mean that you are prepared to journey all the way down to Wimbledon?"

"You make it sound like the North Pole. Just name the time and I'll be there."

After that there was the rigmarole of going through his engagement diary for Wednesday, Thursday, and Friday to demonstrate how busy Jonas was.

"You're certainly keeping your nose to the grindstone," Christopher said. "What about today?"

"Right now?"

"Right now."

"You mean that an important official of the Law Society is prepared to come down to Wimbledon to see me today?"

Christopher said patiently, "It looks as if it's got to be today, or next week. It's up to you."

"Then *of course* we'll make it this afternoon." He was apparently conferring a great favor. "It's number twenty-seven B, Coalporter Street. A few minutes from Wimbledon Station. You won't find it in the Law List. We haven't been here long."

Christopher got there at four o'clock, and thought at first that he must have mistaken the number, since the building which was marked as number 27 appeared to belong entirely to Crompton and Maudling, Surveyors, Auctioneers, and Estate Agents. Then he spotted the plate outside a side door: "Jonas Killey, LL.B. Solicitor and Commissioner for Oaths. Second Floor."

Two flights of linoleum-covered stairs edged with metal ribbing led up to a small landing. A hand-printed notice invited him to Ring and Enter, which he did.

There was a long thin outer office, just large enough to hold two wooden chairs and a table covered with back numbers of the *Law Journal*. On the walls were handbills announcing forthcoming sales by Messrs. Crompton and Maudling, and there was a hatch on the far side with a frosted glass window to it, and a bell on the ledge in front. Beyond it he could hear a typewriter being punished.

He pressed the bell. The typing stopped, the hatch opened, and a middle-aged lady peered out. Christopher told her who he was, and she said would he take a seat as Mr. Killey was temporarily engaged with a client.

None of the walls was very thick. Christopher guessed that he was in what had once been a single large room, now partitioned into three or four. He could hear Jonas' voice. It had an odd nasal twang to it. He seemed to be doing most of the talking. Christopher could hear an occasional mumble and grumble from his client, like a double bass interrupting a long saxophone solo. Then a door beside the hatch opened and they came out.

Jonas was saying, "Really, Mr. Huxtable, you have to understand that there are rules and regulations which a solicitor is bound to observe."

Mr. Huxtable looked as though he didn't give a hoot for rules and regulations but wanted something on the cheap. He departed grumbling. Jonas said, "We shall be about half an hour, Mrs. Warburton. Tell Willoughby he'll have to wait." He held the door open, and Christopher walked into the front part of the office, which commanded a good view of a betting shop on the other side of Coalporter Street and was crammed with the papers, files, books, and paraphernalia which in a larger office might have been kept out of sight.

Jonas waved him to the client's chair, inspected him briefly, and said, "Your hair's going back a lot. If you don't watch it, you'll be bald before you're forty."

"You're not looking any younger yourself," Christopher said.

"If you gentlemen who sit at ease in Chancery Lane had the faintest conception of the work involved in running a solicitor's practice, you would be a trifle more sympathetic to our problems."

"All right. I'm sympathetic. That's why I've come to see you. I gather you want us to pursue your trade union case for you. I've been reading the papers, and I'm bound to say that I think you're plowing the sand."

"Do you now?"

"I don't think any court in the world would order a trade union, which, incidentally, no longer exists, to hold a meeting that took place six years ago all over again because of a technicality which they failed to observe. If it's any consolation to you, I think you were probably quite right. Under the 1964 Act the apprentice members should have been allowed to vote."

"I'm gratified that you grant me that much."

"But have you considered this point? The total number of apprentice members at that date was under fifty."

"Forty-seven to be precise."

"Right. So even if every one of them had voted against amalgamation, it would not have negatived the resolution."

"And you think that is the view the court would take?"

There was something here that Christopher didn't understand. Jonas was not only playing his cards close to his chest, he was playing them as though he had a couple of aces up his sleeve. Christopher said, in a tone that he made intentionally provocative, "I think you'll find that I'm right about that."

"Then that, of course, settles it," said Jonas. "When an official occupying an important position in the Law Society comes to a considered conclusion, there is no more to be said about the matter. Except, of course," he added, "that it is absolutely immaterial. I am no longer concerned with what took place at that particular meeting. I am interested in certain events which took place—or possibly I should say did *not* take place—before and after it. If you would care to cast an eye over these few papers . . ." He walked across to the safe and extracted a folder. Christopher was relieved to see that it was a slim one. "You will then be able to give me your considered opinion on a much more important topic. Should Mr. William Dylan still be at liberty, or should he be serving a short but salutary term of imprisonment?"

The train back to Waterloo, moving against the commuter tide, was slow and almost empty. Christopher was glad of the chance of undisturbed thought. He was trying to make some sense out of what Jonas had told him.

When he got back to the Society, Laurence Fairbrass had gone home. He always slipped away quickly when a test match was being played. He liked to see as much as he could of the last hour's play on television. As soon as stumps had been drawn, Christopher rang him up. He was in a good mood. The England bowlers had been tying up the opposition's tail.

He said, "It sounds to me like just another silly-Killey. It's impossible to tell without seeing the figures."

"He gave me copies of the accounts."

"I'll look at them in the morning. I shouldn't lose any sleep over it if I were you."

"Actually, I don't see why we should worry about it at all," Christopher said. "It's nothing to do with us."

He said the same thing the next morning while Laurence examined the photostats he had brought back with him.

"What are this lot?"

"They're the accounts of ACAT for the six years before the amalgamation."

"ACAT was Dylan's union, wasn't it?"

"Dylan's union is a good description of it. It was a tiny affair. Never more than six hundred members. He was secretary, treasurer, and convener of the shop stewards."

"I can't read the signature on the certificate."

"Jonas says it was an old boy called Mason. He had been a union member before he retired."

"A qualified accountant?"

"Good heavens no. Nothing like that."

Laurence said, "Hmph," and started to read. He spent half his working life studying accounts and could read a balance sheet as easily as someone else could read an ordinary fairy story.

He said, "These seem perfectly straightforward. Member's subscription £3.10 per annum. It doesn't seem a lot."

"Actually it was slightly above the national average at the time."

Laurence looked at Christopher over his glasses and said, "And how would you know that?"

"I looked it up."

"I thought you said this was nothing to do with us."

Christopher hadn't any real answer to that. Laurence was doing sums with a pencil on his blotter. He said, "Income from subscriptions, say £2150. Rents from property £950. What would those be?"

"Some old buffer died and left them a block of shops and offices. The union used one of the offices as its headquarters.

That's why you won't find any figure for rent in the income and expenditure account."

"Outgoings—lighting, heating, rates, insurance, postage, secretarial and audit expenses, representation at congresses, shop stewards' expenses—just under two thousand pounds a year. They didn't waste money, did they?"

"They seem to have run the whole thing on a shoestring," Christopher said. "They were regularly saving over a thousand pounds a year. It all went into the Provident Fund. It was pretty healthy when they joined MG. You can see the figure in the last account, £10,980."

"What *are* these accounts? I mean, who was accounting to who?"

"Dylan, as treasurer, had to account to his own trustees once a year for the money in his hands."

"Not to the registrar?"

"No. They weren't a registered union. They didn't have to make an annual return."

"So these are nothing more than private accounts, circulated inside the family and audited by a member of the family."

"That's correct."

"And Killey says these accounts were fudged?"

"Not a bit of it. They were a bit amateurish, but perfectly accurate as far as they went."

"Then what *is* he saying?"

"To understand that you have to look at MG's annual return. The amalgamation took place in the autumn. The instrument of amalgamation was dated October tenth. On this occasion MG had to split the annual return. You see?"

"I can see that," said Laurence. "They show their own assets separately. They had to do that, I expect, to reconcile them with the previous year's return. And then they show what they took over from ACAT. I imagine in subsequent returns the assets were amalgamated?"

"Right."

"I still don't see the rabbit."

"It's the Provident Fund. In ACAT's June account it was shown as £10,980. In the handover it's down to £10,450. The difference is shown as amalgamation expenses."

"Not unreasonable, surely? Solicitors and accountants involved. It could easily have cost £530."

"There are two points about that," Christopher said. "The first is that ACAT was quite regularly saving about a hundred pounds a month. Between June and October they ought to have been four hundred pounds richer, not five hundred pounds poorer. The other is that ACAT didn't have any amalgamation expenses."

"They didn't?"

"MG paid them all. It was in the agreement. Not many people knew it, but Killey did, because he drafted the agreement himself."

"Didn't someone question this at the time?"

"It wouldn't have been at all easy to spot," Christopher said. "You have to have three separate bits of information. The private June account of ACAT, which only the trustees saw; the annual return of MG, which went to the registrar; *and* a copy of the amalgamation agreement. I don't know who saw that. Probably only the lawyers. It's taken Jonas himself all this time to spot the bug under the chip. All the time that he's wasted beefing about irregularities in voting procedure he could have been making a much more serious allegation against Dylan. Peculation of union funds."

Laurence wasn't listening. He was reading the papers again, considering the figures, puzzling out their significance, weighing probability against improbability, truth against falsehood.

In the end he said, "It's plausible, but I don't think it'll hold water. There are too many unknown factors. For instance, ACAT had been losing members each year. Not many, but the numbers were dropping. Probably that's one reason they were keen to join up with MG. When the news of the amalgamation got about, they could easily have lost more. During the four months between June and October they could have been running at a loss."

"There's nothing to show it either way," Christopher agreed. "I suppose one could find out, if the records still existed."

"Another thing, you know very well that when one party undertakes to pay the costs of a transaction, it never means every penny. It means direct and necessary costs. Dylan could have had a lot of running about to do. Days and even weeks in Sheffield. MG wouldn't have paid for all that."

"Certainly," Christopher said, "and they could have given a farewell dinner to the outgoing trustees. There are lots of possible explanations. All Killey is saying is that, on the face of the accounts, several hundred pounds have gone spare, and it's up to Dylan to explain just where and how they went."

"Why Dylan in particular?"

"Because he was treasurer. And because he had a sole signature on the current account. If any money was extracted, he was the person to do it. And there was something else. He was pretty hard up at the time."

"How do you know?"

"Killey says so. He says that at least one of the local solicitors had a writ out against him. It was a debt to a builder for over two hundred pounds. It was paid off just after the amalgamation. And he thought Dylan had a number of other debts—all of which were paid off at the same time. It didn't bother anyone. The impression was that when MG took him on as assistant secretary they made him a loan, on fairly generous terms, to get his creditors off his neck."

"Which they could have done."

"Which," Christopher agreed, "they could have done."

"But you don't believe it?"

"I don't know what to believe," Christopher said unhappily. "Jonas hates Will Dylan so much that anything he says about him is suspect. If we heard the other side of the story, the whole

14

accusation could easily evaporate into nothing."

"By Hot Air out of Spite," said Laurence. "It's not a horse I'd back myself."

"I think he means business this time."

"He meant business last time."

"Last time there was nothing he could do about it. The only person who can go to the court and complain that the rules have been broken is a member of the union. And Jonas wasn't."

"What about the registrar?"

"The registrar has no power to ensure that a union keeps its own rules."

"Who says so?"

"Mr. Cyril Grunfeld in *Modern Trade Union Law.*"

"I can see we shall have to make you our expert on trade unions," said Laurence sourly. He thought about it for a bit and savaged his spectacles some more. He got through about a pair a year.

"What you're saying is that as this is a criminal offense he can open the bowling himself?"

"All he has to do is to apply to a magistrate for a summons."

"And persuade him to grant it. He mightn't find that so easy."

"Agreed. But just think of the publicity when he tries."

Laurence thought about it and said, "This will have to go up to Tom."

Tom Buller sent for Christopher later that morning. Tom was secretary of the Law Society, which meant that he was the man who runs it. In theory the top brass is the council, but they're working solicitors and they turn up when they can. He is there all the time.

It was a tricky job. The Society was liable to be shot at from three different directions at once. By the public, who think that solicitors charge too much; by the politicians who like to get a few cheap votes by pandering to this view, particularly toward election time; and by the solicitors themselves, who think the Society isn't doing enough to stand up to the public and the politicians. Tom had been at the helm long enough to develop a built-in radar warning of rocks ahead.

He said, "I understand you went to see Jonas Killey yesterday. He's got some complaint about this man Dylan. Can you explain what it is?"

Christopher did his best. Every time he repeated it, it seemed less plausible.

"And he wants us to help him?"

"I think so, yes."

"Didn't he come to us about it before?"

"It was the same man, but not the same complaint. Last time it was a question of the rights and wrongs of the voting at a union meeting. This time it goes a lot further. He's suggesting that Dylan embezzled union funds."

"If he thinks a criminal offense has been committed, he should go to the police. If they won't help him, he can swear out an information himself."

"Yes."

"Then why are we bothering about it? What's it got to do with us?"

One had to be careful with Tom when he asked a question like that. Sometimes he liked to play everything straight down the middle. But every now and then, when one followed that line, one was accused of being stuffy and civil-service minded. You couldn't win.

Christopher said, "He's a solicitor, and it looks to me as if he's going to make a thundering ass of himself. If we could head him off, it would be a good thing for the profession as a whole."

Tom thought about this, moving his lower jaw as though he were chewing Christopher's words into small pieces and getting ready to spit them out. He said, "Law and politics. Oysters and whisky. Both very acceptable on their own. But mix them and you'll get nothing but a sour stomach."

After that he was silent for so long that Christopher thought it was the end of the matter and started to shuffle his papers together. Tom said, "If somebody had to read the riot act to him, who'd be the best person? He wouldn't listen to you—"

Christopher agreed hastily.

"And if *I* did it, it would bring the Society into it officially, which is the last thing I want. Laurence tells me you've got a brother-in-law in Fleet Street who might be able to have a word with Dylan."

"I'm having lunch with him today."

"And what are you hoping to achieve? Except," he added unkindly, "a good lunch at the expense of the Society."

Christopher explained what they had in mind.

Tom said, "It might have worked before this embezzlement thing came up. I don't think it's going to work now. However, it's worth trying. If there is going to be an olive branch, it's got to come from Dylan's side. That's clear."

"Do you think," Christopher said, "that Jonas might listen to Edward Lambard?"

"Lambard," said Tom. "Yes. That's not a bad idea at all. In fact, it's the most sensible thing you've said yet."

Christopher looked gratified. Edward Lambard had been a member of the council for twenty years. When his turn came for president, he had passed the chair, being too busy to give up a whole year's practice. This had meant, incidentally, that he had also passed up the knighthood which went with the job. It hadn't worried him, but it must have been pain and grief to his lady wife. Christopher knew that Tom thought a lot of him.

He said, "You and Killey both worked for Sexton and Lambard once, didn't you?"

"That's right. And they do a lot of semi-political jobs. Trade union, Friendly Society, Employers and Trade Association stuff. They've got a big practice with the Monopolies Commission."

"When you say political . . ." said Tom, wrinkling up his nose again.

"I don't mean they had any particular axe to grind. They were just as ready to argue a union case against the employer as the other way round."

"I think it's quite a good idea," said Tom. He didn't explain which of three different things they had been talking about was a good idea, but Christopher guessed he meant that he was going to talk things over with Edward Lambard. As Christopher was leaving, Tom, who always liked a good curtain line, said, "You'll never understand Killey until you've read Killey Against North West Marine Appliances. It's in the King's Bench reports for 1945 and Appeal Court a year or two later—1948, I think."

Christopher said, "Those dates can't be right, surely. Jonas must still have been a schoolboy in 1945."

"I expect he was," said Tom with a smile. "You look it up."

Patrick Mauger, one of the three lobby correspondents of the *Watchman,* and his brother-in-law Christopher Martingale, with whom he was lunching, were good examples of the danger of judging young men by their outward appearance.

A stranger, told that one of the occupants of the corner table was a radical journalist and the other an institutional solicitor, would almost certainly have miscast them. It was Christopher, the man of law, who had the untidy fair hair and the casual appearance and speech of an undergraduate. Patrick wore his dark hair short, and he affected in business hours the neat blue suit, white shirt, and crisp appearance of a young City tycoon. His speech was equally deceptive. For an occasion such as the present, he adopted the dignified and deliberate diction of an elderly politician, a manner which he dropped completely when playing darts in a public house with his cronies.

"As you know, my dear Christopher," he was saying. "I have very little use for either of our so-called major political parties. I am really a liberal-radical of the old totem." He held up the glass of Mazy Chambertin which he was enjoying at the expense of the Law Society, examined it critically, sniffed its bouquet, and swallowed a mouthful of it. "In my considered opinion, the political scene is a mess. It's a two-horse race, and both the horses must ultimately be losers. The Socialists are lumbered with the unions. Heaven save us from our friends. The Conservatives are weighted out by the Old School Tie."

"All right," said Christopher. "I'll go along with that. It's not a very profound diagnosis. Where does Dylan come into it?"

"Dylan comes into it because he's got a foot in both camps. And because both sides trust him and need him. And my God, how the country needs him."

"You think he's as good as that?"

"I think that if he plays his cards properly he could be Prime Minister by the time he's forty-five. The first Prime Minister since Churchill in 1940 with the country more or less united behind him. If we could get that, we could lick the world. That's why you've got to get someone to strangle Killey." Patrick took another sip of the wine and added, "He ought really to have been strangled at birth."

"Maybe," said Christopher. "But he wasn't. He's right there in Wimbledon. Full of fight."

"This new thing he's got hold of. It's a criminal charge?"

Christopher said, "Yes," but he said it unhappily. He hadn't told Patrick any of the details, but he'd had to give him a general idea.

"Then I suppose it must be embezzlement."

"Look, you mustn't start spreading this round. It's none of it proved, and it's probably libelous."

"Discretion itself," said Patrick earnestly.

Christopher's heart sank. He knew enough about newspapermen to know that they look on an exclusive bit of news like a fox looks at a fat duck.

To change the subject he said, "You've been doing this profile thing. Tell me what you've found out about him."

"His father was a farm worker at a place called Chapel-en-le-Frith, who never earned more than three pounds a week in his life. He had a quiverful of daughters before Will arrived. Will was the only son."

"His Benjamin."

"You'd think they'd have spoilt him. But they're hard-headed folk up north. He went to the local school, like everyone else, and left at fifteen and got a lot of casual jobs, and when he was eighteen he got taken on as a pot hand at ASIA. Perhaps I should explain—"

Christopher said, "ASIA is the Anglo-Scottish Independent Aluminium Company. I know a lot of this story already. But carry on. It's interesting to hear it from the other side."

"ASIA was a grand conception. You know they found big bauxite deposits in Northern Ireland? They came to light during the war, when they were excavating anti-aircraft gun shelters. The supply was cheap and plentiful, and it was easy to ship across to the Mersey. Once it was there, they had unlimited water power from the big Magland and Ladybower reservoirs. And—what was most important of all—they had a market for the stuff. The Midlands were at the start of the postwar boom."

"It all sounds too good to be true."

"It was too good to be safe. The American and Canadian companies, who had the world market in their pocket at that time, decided to freeze it out. They lowered their prices, to rock bottom, and under. They reckoned they were big enough to take a year's loss. Even two years. ASIA wasn't. The management got worried. The banks threatened to withdraw their support."

"I've never understood about bankers," said Christopher. "You'd imagine, from their advertisements, that they were great big resolute father figures all ready to stand up for their struggling little clients. Actually they seem to lose heart quicker than a woman cornered by a mouse."

"They're cold-hearted bastards," said Patrick. "And pretty soon they're going to be nationalized. It's high up on our party program." He helped himself to another mouthful of burgundy. "It wasn't the banks who saved the situation. It was Will Dylan. He was secretary and treasurer and practically everything else at ACAT. When things looked grim, he went to the ASIA management and offered them a deal. He guaranteed that the work force would carry on for two years without asking for any increase in wages. They would even accept a marginal cutting down of numbers, not by sacking men but by slowing recruitment. He'd worked out that if they did this, added to their cheap sources of supply and power, they could reduce the price of their aluminium ingot to a point where the Americans, who were running into labor problems of their own, simply couldn't compete. The other side of the bargain was that when the markets had been reestablished, they would take a three-year rise at the end of the second year. It wasn't quite as simple as that. There were a lot of special grades and hardship clauses and so on. But that's what it amounted to. The management listened to him and did their own sums and arrived at the same answers."

"I can see Dylan convincing the management," Christopher said. "It must have been a hell of a lot more difficult to swing the men."

"It *was* difficult. His strongest card was that he wasn't a visiting union official. He was one of them. He'd worked alongside them in the pot room. He'd got powdered borax in his hair and liquid aluminium on his boots. No one ever called him anything but Will. He barnstormed up and down the works, talking to men singly and in groups and at mass meetings in the canteen. He talked turkey to them. If the Americans took over, they were going to shut half the pot lines and put the other half on specialized production. Three quarters of the men would be made redundant. Which did they prefer? To see three quarters of their mates out of work, or all go on together with a fair chance of coming out square at the end of the day? If the management had said it, the men would have laughed at them

22

and called it a wangle to increase profits. From Will, somehow or other, they took it."

"And it worked?"

"Certainly it worked. As soon as they started making a profit again, the banks recovered their nerve, the company was recapitalized, the workers were properly paid, and Will Dylan became a name of power in the north. I should add that he was just twenty-four at the time."

Christopher thought about it. It seemed to him improbable on the face of it that the man who had done the sort of things his cousin was talking about would have put a few hundred pounds of union funds into his own pocket. The two sides of the portrait didn't match.

"He had a number of union jobs after that," said Patrick. "When MG took over, he became their assistant general secretary, and he was secretary three years later. He didn't hit the national headlines until they made him chairman of the tribunal that arbitrated on the metal workers' dispute. That was a bloody miracle, if you like. No one thought he'd pull it off. The two sides were in entrenched positions, without any apparent room for maneuver. Somehow he wheedled and hectored and bluffed them into moving. Someone who was there said it was mass hypnosis. At the end of ten days they were surprised to find they'd climbed out of their trenches and were shaking hands in no man's land."

"It's a pity he wasn't around in 1914. He might have stopped the war."

"He stopped a very nasty strike, and became a national figure. Both parties were angling for him. Then the member for West Sheffield broke his neck stepping off a train at what he thought was a station and was really a twenty-foot drop into a culvert, and Will saw his chance. It was his home constituency. He stood as an Independent, and romped home."

"He was in luck there," said Christopher. "It was a by-election. That's when personalities pull in votes. At a general election it's the party ticket every time."

"Maybe. My guess is he'd have got in at a general election. But I agree he'd have had to declare his allegiance in advance. As it was, he reached Westminster without any precommitment, which not many people have done since they abolished the university vote."

"And as soon as he got there, he accepted the government whip."

"That was sensible too. He couldn't have done much on his own. What you've got to understand about Dylan is that he's a practical man. He doesn't believe in shouting slogans or nailing doctrinaire colors to the mast or laying down a lot of rules as though politics was a game of county cricket."

Christopher said, "That sounds like a sentence out of your profile, Patrick."

Patrick had the grace to blush. He said, "I'd back a man like Dylan every time, because whatever methods he uses, his motives are sound. He believes in equality of opportunity. And so do I. Do you think we could get a third glass out of that bottle?"

The discussion was on the point of disappearing into the mists of politics armed by the red glow of wine. Christopher dragged it back ruthlessly. "What we want you to do, is to slip in a word next time you have a session with Dylan. Tell him that a small olive branch might be a good investment."

"I couldn't possibly say that."

"Why not?"

"It's a mixed metaphor."

"Don't be tiresome. You know what I mean. He's a big man, and you say he's a practical man. Jonas is a small man, and a copper-bottomed crank with an obsession. I believe that all he really wants is a gesture of reconciliation. Couldn't Dylan slip in a word in one of his interviews with you? Say that he realizes now that Jonas was technically correct—"

"I'll try," said Patrick. "But if Killey's going to press criminal charges, it will be almost impossible for Dylan to climb down.

If he did, wouldn't he be admitting that he was guilty?"

Christopher said, "You've got to do something to justify that burgundy."

"It was a lovely wine," agreed Patrick. "I've got a date with Dylan at the House at four o'clock. Do you think we've got time for a glass of port?"

Will Dylan said, "The way you spell it out, amalgamation's a dirty word. That's the message, is it?"

"It's not the amalgamation. It's the jobs we lose, lad," said Jacob Hooker. He was the leader of the deputation and vice-chairman of the West Sheffield constituency association.

"All right, Jacob. Let's look at it that way. Two firms get together. Some of the jobs overlap. Some men are made redundant. But the joint firm's more efficient. Increases its turnover, grabs more of the market. Takes the extra men back, but uses them properly."

"There's no guarantee of that," snapped the thin man who sat next to Jacob. The right sleeve of his jacket was pinned to the lapel. He had lost an arm when an overhead conveyor belt had slipped and dropped a hundredweight of scrap metal onto his right shoulder.

"Nothing's certain in this life, Martin. But I'll make you a forecast. You take two firms that are too small to be really efficient. They're up against competitors who are bigger and better organized. What's going to happen to them?"

He looked at the eight men who were sitting around the table. None of them said anything.

"You know as well as I do. You've all seen it happen. They stagger on for a year or two, piling up losses. Then they fold up. Their machinery's sold for scrap. Their men are out of a job. Not just a few of them, Martin. The lot. Look what happened when Warfields wanted to join up with Cunningham and Bennet. It might have worked. I don't say it would have. But it had a chance. As soon as it was even whispered about, you had the

Warfields men out on strike. You know what the pickets had on their banners? 'Protect Our Jobs.' I saw them. I'd have laughed if I hadn't been crying. Well, that strike was effective. Very effective indeed. It put Warfields right out of business and lost six hundred jobs. Now Cunningham and Bennet want to join up with Tolbury's. Are we going to have the same thing all over again?"

"I can see the sense of that," said Hooker. "I mean, speaking personally, I can see the sense of it. But it's not easy to get it across to the people who are going to lose their jobs. You say, *when* the joint firm gets cracking and *when* it makes more money and expands, some of the men are going to get their jobs back. Right? But that's a year or two ahead. It's what they bring home *now* that pays the bills."

There was a growl of agreement around the table. Almost all the men there had known what it was to be out of work, to be let down with a bump from a working wage to a social security payment which barely covered the needs of their families.

"All right," said Dylan. "It comes down to cases. I'll go up and talk to the management. But I'm not going to talk a lot of hot air. We want a list of people who would be made redundant. Not by numbers. By names. And we need to know what the management is going to do for them. Whether it can place them anywhere else. How far it can supplement the state benefits until they get fixed."

"We don't want any lump sum payments," said Martin. "We all know what happens to golden handshakes. Four Saturday evenings at the local, and it's all back in the pockets of the brewers."

"Right," said Dylan. "Compensation for loss of the job, but spread over six months. We shall have to fix it so that it doesn't cut down the social security."

"Six months? Is that long enough?"

"I'd reckon so. You've got to remember that it won't be floor workers who go. They'll be operating the same number of smelters and reduction plants after the amalgamation as they were before. It's the overheads and administration they'll be saving on—maintenance men, telephonists, and office staff. People like that don't find it too difficult to get fixed."

"The people who'll get fixed quickest," said Martin, "are the typists. They're getting it with cream and jam. My daughter's a typist. First week she went to work she was earning more'n I did after twenty years on the floor."

The conversation turned to grades and differentials. Dylan, who had been looking at his diary, said, "I can't make it up north till next Monday. I'll see you all then. We've got to pack it up now. There's a newspaperman waiting outside for me to tell him what a bloody fine chap I am."

"You want to watch it," said Hooker. "They'll twist your words. The other day I had one of them ask me what I thought of our chairman. He had me down as saying that I thought he was a grand old buster—would you credit it? What I really said was he was a randy old bastard."

Dylan found Patrick Mauger sitting patiently in the corridor outside the conference room. A group of ladies wearing tight hats and horn-rimmed glasses were waiting to go in and tell the Junior Undersecretary of State for Education what was wrong with the nation's nursery schools. A member who was shepherding a party of his constituents down the corridor had met head-on with a group of Middle Eastern journalists. A worried-looking government whip was dodging about in the crowd like a scrum half looking for an opening. He was muttering to himself. Maybe he was saying his prayers.

"It's a bloody miracle," said Dylan, "that this outfit functions at all. It's overcrowded and understaffed, and if you try to change anything they just look at you and say, 'Oh, we've *always* done it this way.' Any business that tried to operate like that would be bankrupt in a month."

"People like it," said Patrick. "If Parliament was too well organized, they'd think it was totalitarian. Who are those boys you were seeing? They looked a tough crowd."

"I'll tell you about them in the car. I'm getting off home for a breather."

They made their way out to the forecourt where members' cars were parked. The "A" Division sergeant on the door knew them both and nodded. Patrick's work took him often enough to the House for him to be on terms with most of the officials and policemen.

"We four departmental undersecretaries share this car," said Dylan, "and as I'm the new boy I don't see much of it, do I, Tom?"

The uniformed chauffeur grinned and said, "Where to, sir? Home?"

"Home's the word," said Dylan.

The streets were fairly empty, and it took them less than ten minutes to reach the Embankment end of the Albert Bridge and another five to get aboard Dylan's floating home, one of the colony of houseboats moored at Chiswick Ait.

"I've been loaned this floating palace by a chap in the Foreign Service," said Dylan. "He got posted to Lima. A bit of luck for me. I shouldn't have been able to afford to bring my family down to London without it."

"You've got them all here then?"

"The Dylan family is complete again: wife Pauline, eldest son Paul, daughter Ellen, and a young bombshell called Fred. Six years old and more trouble than all the others put together."

"And your favorite."

"How did you guess," said Dylan with a grin. "Watch the gangplank, or you'll be in the drink. Fred's fallen in three times already. I think he does it on purpose. You'll stop and have some tea with us, I hope. Pauline, come and meet the press."

Pauline Dylan was a woman in her early thirties, some six or seven years younger than her husband. A woman of some character, Patrick guessed, neither out of the top nor the bottom drawer, but out of that very large middle drawer of an increasingly classless northern society. He was not surprised when he discovered later on that she had started life in the cottage of a mill hand and had got a First in Sociology at Leeds University. Four years as the wife of an M.P. had hardened her to unexpected visitors.

She said, "Come along in. I hope you realize, Mr.—"

"Mauger. Patrick Mauger."

"Mr. Mauger, that when a Yorkshire woman says 'tea' she doesn't mean thin bread and butter and cakes."

"Whatever she means is all right by me," said Patrick.

They went into the main room, which had a big stern window and a view across the river which Whistler would have approved of.

"I was complaining to you about the old-fashioned habits of Parliament," said Dylan. "I believe that its timetable was designed for a period when a gentleman dined at five or six in the evening and took supper around midnight. Can you eat sausages, Patrick?"

"Just try me," said Patrick.

When a substantial high tea had been disposed of, Dylan said, "You were asking about those men I was seeing this afternoon. They're fine people. A bit truculent, because they're worried. But it's their folk they're worried about, not themselves. Out of the eight men there, I happen to know that four of them paid their own fares to come down here and talk to me. All right, it's a small thing. But how many businessmen would have made the journey without charging it to expenses?"

"Very few," said Patrick. "What's worrying them?"

"It's hard times for the copper recovery plants."

"Recovery?"

"There's a lot of copper lying about. Obsolete and discarded machinery and equipment. Anything made of copper's worth melting down and using again. The business really got under way during the war, when we couldn't ship in the raw material. Even in America, where they can dig the stuff out of the ground, nearly a fifth of their output is secondary production. Didn't you know?"

"What I don't know about the copper industry could be put into several large books," said Patrick. "Go on, what happened next?"

He wasn't writing anything down. He had found that the sight of someone taking notes inhibited good talk. He retained the essentials of what he was told by a system of mental mnemonics. Most newspapermen acquire this knack.

"What happened next was what always happens when there's a good thing going. Too many people climbed on the bandwagon. A lot of little firms started up, without enough capital behind them, and made a bit of easy money. When the going became harder the option was to fold up altogether or amalgamate. Common sense said amalgamate. Save some jobs instead of losing all of them. But it wasn't an easy idea to put across. Because when two firms got together, they saw the directors all getting cushy jobs in the joint outfit, or a bloody good golden handshake if they had to go; while as far as the work force was concerned, it was 'Thank you very much. Don't bother to turn up on Monday.' I cut my teeth on problems like that when I was in ACAT, and had a lot more of it when I went over to MG."

"That was one of the things I wanted to ask you about," said Patrick. "Didn't you have a bit of bother when the two unions joined up?"

"Bother?"

"With a chap called Killey."

"Ah," said Dylan. "Him. Yes, I did have a bit of trouble with him. You remember that chap, Pauline?"

"I remember you bawling him out," said Mrs. Dylan, who had come back into the room to clear the dishes. "I always said you made a mistake there."

"You could be right, love. I ought to have patted him on the back instead of kicking him on the bottom, but I was younger then."

"It would have saved you a heap of trouble."

"It would have saved me writing about two hundred letters," agreed Dylan.

"Would it be a good idea to do something like that now?"

Dylan looked surprised and said, "I haven't seen him for years. Don't say he's starting up again."

"It's not so much starting up again. He seems to be on a new tack."

"What's it this time?"

"Last time he was on about voting. This time it's something to do with money."

"For God's sake! Whose money? His or mine or the union's?"

"I don't completely understand what it's about," said Patrick. He was finding it difficult to say in cold blood, "Someone thinks you're a thief."

"If he thinks Will's had a penny that wasn't his," said Pauline, "he's mad. Not just bad, mad. He wants certifying."

"You must have some idea what it's about," said Dylan.

Patrick said, "It's something to do with the amalgamation. My brother-in-law knows about it. He works for the Law Society, and he got it from Killey. Come to think of it," he added with a grin, "I promised him I wouldn't tell anyone, but he can't have meant you."

"If he's going about saying things like that," said Dylan grimly, "I certainly ought to know about it. Politics is a game where any mud sticks."

"If he says it in public," said Pauline, "you've got to do something about it, Will. It's libelous, isn't it?"

"I think he's got enough sense to realize that," said Patrick. "He's a lawyer himself."

"Do *you* think I ought to do something about it?"

"The original idea was that if you made a friendly gesture of some sort, he might accept the olive branch and pipe down. I quite see that you can't do that until he withdraws the present suggestion."

"It wouldn't have worked any old way," said Dylan. "I've done a lot of negotiating in my time, and I've got to know something about the way people's minds work. One sort of chap, you give him a little and he's grateful and he gives you a bit back, and sooner or later you meet in the middle. But there's another sort. You give him something, he doesn't say thank you. As far as he's concerned, you've gone back and he's gone forward. It's a new start line."

"You think Killey's like that?"

"He comes from Grantham. If there's anyone more obstinate than a Yorkshireman it's a Fenman."

The conversation turned onto families and backgrounds, and Patrick kept it there until it was time for him to go.

After he had gone, Dylan said, "Bugger Killey. Why should we let him spoil our lives for us. I'll give you a hand with the dishes."

Over the washing-up Pauline said, "You'll have to do something about Fred. He cut school again today."

"Cut it?"

"He said he had a headache and they sent him home. Only he didn't come home. He'd been promised a trip by the river police. They took him down to Wapping in one of their launches."

Dylan started to laugh, turned it into a cough, and said, "There's not much I can do about that, love."

"You'll have to take your hand to him."

"My father used to take a belt to me," said Dylan, "but it never did me an ounce of good."

"Ninety-four," said Lefty Marks. The way he said it, it sounded like a prayer.

"Three eighteens, double top, Patrick."

"Treble twenty and seventeens, boy."

"Three sixteens, fourteen, double sixteen, boy. Never fails."

"Let the boy work it out for himself."

Patrick took a deep breath. This was a moment to live for. One leg apiece, and ahead by a whisker in the final. Toe up to the brass telltale. Steady as you go. He flipped the heavy dart at the board. Double eighteen.

Got to go for the double top. If he hit it, that left him two nines. Good enough. One of his better numbers. On the other hand, if he missed it and got a single twenty, which was all too likely, it meant a shot at double nineteen. Marks had next throw. Being left-handed he preferred the right-hand side of the board and would find double nineteen awkward.

The computer which lives inside the human head and is more efficient than any man-made computer had these calculations and human equations worked out and analyzed in the time it took him to raise the second dart to eye level. At the very last moment, almost as it left his hand, he changed his aim and went for the single eighteen.

After that double top. Must be. Right in the middle. No argument.

"I don't know what we should do without you, Patrick," said Marks. "Honest I don't. One thing they did teach you at Oxford and Cambridge. How to play darts."

Patrick accepted the pint of beer which was offered to him by his opposite number on the *Daily Telegraph* team. The occasion was an important one. It was the semi-final of the Beaverbrook Cup and the saloon bar of the Marquis of Anglesey was packed to suffocation with players, officials, supporters and plain old-fashioned drinkers.

Patrick felt relaxed and happy. Part of his happiness came from the fact that he was the only man in the *Watchman* contingent from the editorial floor. The rest of the players and supporters were from the works. Compositors, like Edgecombe and Sivewright; Parsons, who was in charge of transport; Marks, who was a senior electricity charge hand and said to be a card-carrying member of the Communist Party.

"Wossit feel like to be in the finals, eh?" said Parsons, fighting his way across with another trayful of pint glasses. "I ordered these before you threw, Patrick. Knew you'd do it."

"Who's the opposition?"

"The *Express*. They think the cup belongs to them, seeing their gaffer gave it."

"Right now," said Patrick, "I feel we could wipe the floor with anyone."

"Mustn't forget they've got Pearly Deans. Semi-final in the *News of the World* last year. Beaten by that Welsh bugger—what was his name—he won it."

No one could remember his name.

Edgecombe, who had the mournful look which all compositors seem to wear like a uniform, said, "He's hot stuff, is Pearly, but there's one thing he can't abide. Band music. Puts him right off his shot."

"And just what are we supposed to do about that?" said Marks. "Hire a bloody great brass band and get it to play outside the window. Look a bit pointed, wouldn't it?"

"What we could do," said Parsons, "is have a bit of band music tape-recorded. Bring in one of those miniature sets, see, and turn it on accidental when he's going for his double out."

Patrick, who had finished his victory pint and was starting work on a follow-up, lost the thread of this interesting discussion. Over his fourth pint he found himself wedged up in one corner with Lefty Marks.

Marks said, "How's the old profile going along, Patrick?"

"It's going all right," said Patrick.

"He's a fine boy. Worth more than most of the silly sods we waste print on."

"He's had an interesting career. I only hope no one tries to spoil it."

"Is someone trying?"

"I'm not sure. I had lunch today with my brother-in-law. He works in the Law Society. He told me something, mind you there's probably nothing in it. He'd got some idea into his head . . ."

Marks listened, bending forward so as not to miss anything and nodding his head from time to time.

The celebrations finished with closing time. The members of the *Watchman* staff who had been given the evening off for the occasion went home to bed. Patrick made his way back to his bachelor flat in Albany Street. As he was undressing, it did occur to him fleetingly to wonder if he might have been a bit indiscreet in what he had said to Marks, but he dismissed the thought. Lefty was all right. He was a good chap.

At that precise moment Marks was making a telephone call. He dialed a Clerkenwell number and was answered, in a cheerful and wide-awake voice, by someone he addressed as Syd. There must have been a dual connection at the other end, because sometimes it was Syd who spoke, and sometimes some-one called Ben. Marks seemed to know both of them well.

When Christopher went home that evening, he remembered what Tom Buller had told him and took with him the King's Bench reports for 1945 and the Appeal cases for 1947.

The weather prophets had predicted that it was going to be the hottest summer of the century, and it was getting off to a good start. The carriage was too crowded for comfortable read-ing, so he saved the reports for study after supper.

Mutt was on the platform to meet him. Why his wife should have been called Mutt was a family mystery. There was a theory that it was a corruption of Mattie or Matilda and that she had earned this name either by telling outrageous lies or because she once set her nursery on fire. She had brought Toby, their one-year-old son, with her, tucked up in a wicker basket on the back seat of the car. Toby was cutting his first tooth and seemed to be resenting it.

After supper, when Toby had at last been induced to go off to sleep, Christopher got out the two reports and read them.

Mutt said, "What's it all about?"

"It's about Jonas' father."

"Jonas again. Why can't you leave him alone?"

"I wish I could," said Christopher.

"What did his father do?"

"It seems he discovered a method of welding which worked efficiently under water. Something to do with electrically in-duced heat and a special flux. I believe everyone uses it now, but it was a novelty then, and commercially very valuable be-cause it meant you could repair an underwater structure with-out hauling the whole thing out."

"And Jonas' father actually invented it?"

"There doesn't seem much doubt about that. He was the

original home-grown boffin. He thought it all up himself and carried out the experiments in his own tool shed. Then he sold it to a crowd called North West Marine Appliances."

"Who tried to steal it from him. Typical."

"That was the general idea. But it wasn't completely one-sided. The company had certainly put a lot of money into developing it and they had an agreement—"

"Drawn up by their own lawyers."

"That's right."

Mutt snorted. Christopher said, "It wasn't crooked. It was just badly worded. The company said it meant the inventor got a sizable lump sum and a limited royalty. Killey senior said it meant that he had the option to take a smaller down payment and a continuing and escalating royalty. Since the thing was a roaring success the royalty was obviously much the sounder bet."

"So they went to court about it, and the only people who made any money out of it were the lawyers."

"Wrong again," said Christopher. "The person who made money was old man Killey. He lost in King's Bench, but he was a sticker. He took it on to Appeal and had a hell of a fight, which must have cost him every penny he had. There was no legal aid in those days, remember, and at the end of the day he came out on top, with costs in both courts, and a fat royalty. His widow has been living on it ever since."

"His widow?"

"That was the sad part about it. The fight seems to have taken too much out of him. He died a few months after the case was over."

Mutt said, "Hmph," and was clearly on the point of drawing a moral from this tale when Toby started up again and side-tracked her.

Dylan said, "I think you ought to know, Minister, that there might be some trouble coming up."

Bernard Gracey was Minister for Labor at that time. He was the man who dropped the famous clanger at question time in the House. The honorable member for somewhere-or-other had asked him how many apprentice pottery hands there were in Staffordshire and how many years it took for them to qualify as potters. Reading rather hurriedly from the slip of paper in his hand, he had said, "The answer to the first question is five and to the second question is 6750." This had tickled the sense of humor of the members, which rarely rises above schoolboy level, and the press had started referring to him as Potter Gracey. It was the sort of fatuous thing which a member never seems to live down. It hadn't done his prospects much good.

The relationship between a boss on the way down and a subordinate on the way up can be prickly, but Dylan seemed to get on with him well enough.

The Minister listened to him courteously and said, "Really, it all seems pretty indefinite. That chap Killey is a bit of a crank, I believe. Didn't he have a bee in his bonnet about some trade union amalgamation? Remind me about that." When Dylan had reminded him, the Minister said, "A pity. There's not a lot one can do to prevent people bringing unfounded charges. A libel action usually does more harm than good. All the same, it could be awkward just at this moment."

Dylan looked at him quickly. The coming election was already casting a shadow. That October or the following March were the only real alternatives. The decision would have to be taken soon.

He said, "At least it's good of you, Minister, to assume that the charges are unfounded."

"I've known you long enough to be certain of that," said Gracey.

When Dylan had gone, he sat thinking about it for quite a long time. Then he picked up the telephone and asked for a number. It was a number which was manned twenty-four hours a day but which did not feature in any telephone directory or listing, public or private. The people who knew it were expected to memorize it, not to write it down.

A few minutes later he was talking to someone he addressed as Toby.

Air Vice-Marshal Toby Pulleyne, D.S.O., D.F.C., was one of those men whom everyone knew but no one knew much about. Although he had been some years retired, he retained an office in the Ministry of Defense. He could be found in the bar of the United Service Club before lunch and at White's in the evening. After that, being a bachelor and excellent company, he usually had a dinner engagement. He was particularly useful to hostesses in the Foreign Office circuit who had to entertain guests from abroad. He spoke two foreign languages well and half a dozen others quite adequately.

The Air Vice-Marshal switched on a tape recorder when Bernard Gracey started talking. When he had finished, he said, "Seems a lot of balls to me, old man. Do you think I'd better have a word with Dylan? I met him once at a City dinner. Made a bloody good speech. Told all the old stuffed shirts where they got off. And my God how they lapped it up."

"That sounds like our Will. I'd be obliged if you would have a word with him. Get some of the details and look into it. We don't want any trouble, particularly just now."

"See what I can do," said Toby Pulleyne.

Other men were on the move that morning. Syd Marvin and Ben Thomas came up by Underground from Clerkenwell to Waterloo and went by British Rail from Waterloo out to Wimbledon. As midday struck, they were ringing the bell in Jonas Killey's waiting room.

Mrs. Warburton cast an experienced eye over them but could come to no conclusion. Not quite seedy enough for process servers. Too cheerful for debt collectors. But not quite the sort of client the firm catered for.

"Would it be a property matter?"

"Just say private business, love," said Ben.

"Mr. Killey only really sees people by appointment."

"Perhaps he'll do us a favor this time," said Syd.

"I'll inquire."

"You do that," said Ben, and he winked at her.

They helped themselves to copies of the *Law Journal* and settled themselves down with the air of men who understood how to wait. Mrs. Warburton retired defeated.

Jonas was, in fact, busy. He was putting the finishing touches to the application which he was due to make in person on the following morning before Mr. Cedric Lyon in the West London Magistrates Court. There were documents to be referred to, and four copies had to be available of each. One for the magistrate, one for his clerk, one for Jonas himself, and one for his opponent, should he choose to appear.

There was also the opening speech to be considered. Jonas had written it and rewritten it half a dozen times. He fancied that he now had it right. Not offensive, but by no means subservient. A free-born Englishman insisting on his rights.

40

"*Who* are they?"

"They wouldn't say, Mr. Killey."

"They didn't give you any idea?"

"They just said it was private business."

"Couldn't Willoughby deal with them?"

"He's doing a completion."

"All right. I suppose I'd better see them."

"Up to you."

"We don't want to turn away business, Mrs. Warburton, do we?"

Mrs. Warburton sniffed but retreated. She soothed her feelings by taking five minutes to finish typing the document in her machine before opening the hatchway and saying, "You can go in now."

Jonas Killey took stock of his visitors. He too found them difficult to place. They were neither smartly nor shabbily dressed. Passing them in the street, he would have put them down as clerks or subordinate employees, but there was something in their faces, and in their voices, which contradicted this, a hint of self-possession, a suggestion of veiled authority.

"And what can I do for you, gentlemen?"

The thinner and more serious of the men, who had introduced himself as Marvin, said, "Thanks for seeing us, Mr. Killey. We'll try not to take up too much of your time."

Thomas said, "Mind if we smoke?" He was shorter, thick rather than fat, and had the sort of face which can be seen in thousands any winter Saturday on the terraces of Cardiff Arms Park.

"Certainly," said Jonas. "I don't myself, but go ahead."

"Sure it doesn't worry you?"

"Not a bit."

Marvin said, "We heard you were having a bit of trouble— perhaps trouble's the wrong word—a bit of business with a character called Dylan."

Jonas stared at him.

41

"Now don't jump the gun," said Thomas. "We're not going to ask you to give away any professional secrets. Right, Syd?"

"That's right, Ben."

"What we came along to say was this. We know all about Will Dylan. He's quite a character. Wouldn't you say so, Syd?"

"I'd say he was quite a character."

"If what we heard is true—and I only say if, because you can never really tell—and you've got something you're trying to pin on him, then it occurred to Syd and me that you might need some help."

"By help," said Marvin, "we don't only mean money. We mean help in getting hold of documents, getting evidence, that sort of thing."

"We're friendly characters," said Thomas. "People talk to us, you'd be surprised."

Jonas, who had made a number of attempts to break into this extraordinary duologue, managed it at last. He said, "Would you mind explaining a couple of things. First of all, who are you? Secondly, how did you get this information about my private business?"

"First question first, Ben?"

"Right, Syd."

Marvin extracted a card from his wallet and laid it on the desk.

Jonas picked it up and read it. He said, "The Workers League for Peace. I'm afraid I've never heard of it."

"We blush unseen," said Marvin. "Down in Clerkenwell. Right, Ben?"

"Like roses on a manure heap," agreed Thomas.

"Or pike in a fish pond," suggested Marvin. As he said this, he smiled for the first time and exposed as he did so a set of sharp and blackened teeth.

"Could we stop talking in riddles," said Jonas. "I repeat, I've never heard of this organization, of which you, Mr. Marvin"— he peered down at the card—"are secretary, and you, Mr. Thomas?"

"Assistant secretary."

"So it really takes us no further, does it?"

"Not a lot," said Thomas. He did not seem upset about it.

"Now perhaps you'll answer my second question. How do you know that I am . . . am contemplating . . . a certain line of action against Dylan. And in any case, what has it got to do with you?"

"If what we heard's right," said Marvin, "and he's been up to some sort of fiddle with union funds, that's something we're naturally concerned about."

"Interests of the workers," said Thomas. "You must see that."

"I see nothing of the sort," said Jonas, rising to his feet. "I see only that someone has been making totally unauthorized statements about something which is entirely my own business. And now, if you don't mind, I'm extremely busy this morning."

"Sure you can handle it yourself?" said Marvin.

"Quite sure, thank you."

"Keep the card. You never know, you might need help. We've got a lot of friends. Midlands, up north, all over the place."

Jonas stared at him for a moment and then said rather stiffly, "I should, I suppose, thank you for coming."

"No need to thank us," said Thomas. "It's our job. Interests of the working classes. Right, Syd?"

"That's right, Ben. We must let the gentleman get on with his work now."

After they had gone, Jonas went back to his chair and sat down. The papers he had been working on were spread all over the desk. It occurred to him that the stouter of his two visitors, who had sat alongside the desk, must have been able to read them. Probably it didn't matter. They seemed to know a lot about it already. Odd couple. Like an old-fashioned comedy duo. Not entirely funny though.

Edward Lambard knocked half an inch of gray ash off his cigar into the end of a twenty-five-pounder cartridge case which served as an ashtray on Tom Buller's desk and said, "Extraordinary story. I don't know that I'm entirely surprised though. Killey is an unusual man."

"He used to work for you, didn't he?"

"He was with us for four years. He was very nearly a very good solicitor indeed."

"Meaning?"

"I mean that he had a hard core of obstinacy which is very necessary in our trade. Give him a case which could be fought, and he'd fight it like a tiger. No. Tiger's the wrong animal. What's the obstinate creature that never lets go?"

"A bulldog."

"Not a bulldog. No. A mongoose. I always thought of Jonas as a mongoose. Bottle brush tail and pink eyes. And the bigger the cobra, the harder he'd bite. I very nearly offered him a partnership."

"But you didn't?"

"In the end, no. There was something missing. Balance. Judgment. The ability to compromise when the interests of the client demanded a compromise."

"Did you know about this Dylan business?"

"I knew he was pursuing a private vendetta of some sort. I didn't know the details. This embezzlement idea is something new, I gather."

"It's new," said Buller. "And it's a great deal more dangerous than the old line. It's a criminal offense, and nothing can stop Killey applying for a summons. If Dylan were a nobody, it wouldn't signify. I don't think he'll get his summons. Cedric Lyon plays everything by the book. He'll find plenty of reasons for refusing it. But that's not the point. The press will get wind of it, and win or lose, it's not going to do Dylan any good."

"Or Killey."

"That's my view."

Lambard thought about the matter. He was a shortish man, running to stoutness, with an aggressive mustache and an attractively bent nose, the result of a misadventure in the boxing ring in his youth. His hair was gray, but he still had plenty of it; and he had kept most of his own teeth. He wore glasses for reading the small print on his clients' contracts.

He said, "What do you want me to do?"

"If Killey will listen to anyone, he'll listen to you. He thinks a lot of you. I know that."

"I didn't sack him," agreed Lambard. "We parted quite amicably. He might listen to me. I rather doubt it. I don't think I could chase after him."

"But if he came to you, you'd do your best."

"Certainly. Tell me one thing. What's your interest in this?"

Buller thought about that one for a long minute in silence. Then he said, "I believe that the law is the most important thing in the world today. I don't mean the practice of lawyers. I mean the law itself. Normally I sleep well. If there's one thing that can keep me awake at night it's a vision I sometimes have of this country being ruled by the whim of its rulers and not by the rule of law."

"Could that happen here?"

"Of course it could. It's too bloody easy for a government to panic and set the law on one side *because it happens to be inconvenient.* Temporarily, of course. They always mean to bring it back again—some time."

Lambard looked at his old friend in mild surprise and said, "And just where does Killey come into all this?"

"He comes into it because one of the things which helps the process along nicely is when people start to despise or dislike lawyers as a class. What people are going to see here is a solicitor pursuing a legalistic vendetta, apparently out of spite, against a well-liked member of the government. The man in the street may not be great on principles, but personalities are things he can get hold of."

"You may be right." Lambard killed the end of his cigar and said, "Blast Killey. Why can't he keep his mouth shut and get on with his job?"

The Prime Minister looked at Bernard Gracey over the top of the half-moon spectacles which the cartoonists had adopted as his trademark. It was not the first time that he had doubted whether Gracey was the right man for the job. He was clever, and adaptable, but a Minister for Labor needed more than cleverness and adaptability. He needed guts. More, like Napoleon's generals, he needed luck. Gracey had been unlucky on more than one occasion. If they got a reasonable majority at the next election, he would be tempted to give Gracey's job to Dylan. It would be an exceptional promotion, but there were precedents for it.

He said, "Our organization people tell me that Will Dylan is worth thirty or forty seats to us. Partly by luck, partly by judgment, he's become a sort of talisman. There are plenty of marginal constituencies in the Midlands and the north where the unpolitical elector, the 'don't know and don't much care,' the man who wins or loses every election, will say, 'If Will's on their side, they can't be as black as they're painted.' "

"I realize that," said Gracey.

"What have you done about it?"

Gracey hesitated. There were certain things you told the old man, and other things which you didn't tell him, because it might be better for him to be able to disclaim knowledge of them at a later stage. The fact that he might have to disclaim you into the bargain was a risk you took.

He said, "I mentioned the matter to Pulleyne."

"Pulleyne?" said the Prime Minister irritably. "I can't see what it's got to do with him. He's something in Intelligence, isn't he?"

Gracey nearly said, "You ought to know. You appointed him yourself," but discretion prevailed. He gathered that this was to be an occasion on which the right hand had no idea what the left hand was doing. He said, "I thought he might be helpful, Prime Minister. Probably I was quite wrong."

At half past two that afternoon Toby Pulleyne came out of the front door of the United Service Club into the strong sunlight. As he descended the Duke of York's Steps, an American lady said to her daughter, "Now isn't that just a typical English gentleman." Her daughter said, "I've certainly seen his picture in the papers, Mom. Do you think he might be Lord Mountbatten?" Her mother said no. Lord Mountbatten didn't have a gray mustache. She said it regretfully. It would have been very agreeable to her sense of the fitness of things if she had been able to tell the folks back home that she had seen Lord Mountbatten descending the Duke of York's Steps.

Unconscious of the impression he had caused, Pulleyne proceeded on his way across St. James's Park, up the Cockpit Steps, and into Queen Anne's Gate. He was making for Petty France, that curious by-road that curls like an old snake asleep between Buckingham Gate and St. James's Park Underground Station, and seems to be dedicated to the memory of the Iron Duke. One side is flanked by Wellington Barracks. Its two public houses commemorate his victories. The side streets are named after his generals. The second side turning on the left is Picton Street, and a few yards along this stands the square graystone building, considered sizable in its day but now dwarfed by its neighbors, named Lynedoch House after the victor of the battle of Barrossa.

Pulleyne reached it at ten minutes to three, greeted the hall porter as an old friend, and took the lift to the fourth floor, which was wholly occupied by the offices of the Civil Service Special Medical and Welfare Unit.

The organization which had its headquarters at that time on the fourth floor of Lynedoch House was not a large one. Five or six rooms were adequate for its carefully screened employees. It was primarily a communications center, with private lines to the Home Office, the Foreign Office, the Special Branch, the Passport Office, and the headquarters of Customs and Excise at Kings Beam House; also to the officer in charge of the mobile reserve in Wellington Barracks, the government telephone-tapping center at Chelsea, and other less publicized departments of the executive.

The head of the unit at this time was Simon Benz-Fisher. He had taken over when his predecessor was booted out for failing to anticipate and deal with the Christine Keeler affair. That Benz-Fisher had survived in this particular post was a tribute first to his ingenuity and secondly to his ability to think quickly and adapt his plans to the requirements of the moment. These were talents which his training as a barrister had implanted and developed. Before his name disappeared from the Law List, he had been a promising junior Treasury counsel in a chambers which handled a great deal of criminal work. He dressed well, had a head of thick black curly hair on which he balanced a bowler hat, exactly one size too small and purchased new each year from Lock's in St. James's Street. His voice was high, without being in the least effeminate.

He listened carefully to what Pulleyne had to say, making no notes. When he was quite sure that his visitor had no more to tell him, he said, "We've got a file on Killey. It's not a very big one. He's been a minor nuisance. He published an article in a legal journal three years ago commenting on the voting procedure under the 1964 Trade Union Act, with a clear implication that Dylan had had a hand in ballot rigging. There was a question of whether he ought to be sued for libel. That was what Killey was hoping for, of course. He was trailing his coat. We said no."

"It may not be so easy to head him off this time," said Pulleyne.

"He comes up in front of Cedric Lyon. He won't get much change out of him."

"The press will get hold of it."

"If the application is turned down, they'll have to watch their step. It'll be a simple statement of the fact that the application was made and refused. I don't think they'll dare go any further than that."

"Then you don't think any action is called for?"

"Unless you're suggesting that I have Killey tied up in a sack and dumped in the Thames, it's difficult to see what action would be really effective."

"I wasn't making any suggestions," said Pulleyne. "I was presenting you with a problem."

When he had left, Benz-Fisher pressed a bell and a man came in through the communicating door. He said, "You heard all that, Terence?"

"Yes. I heard it." It was a rule of the office that when Benz-Fisher had a visitor anything that was said to him must be heard by a third person. Pulleyne had been aware of this too. "Are we going to do anything about it?"

"I'm not sure."

"It sounded like a lot of balls. A lawyer making a fuss about some small thing to get himself a lot of cheap publicity."

"That's your view of the matter, is it Terence?"

The little man said, "Well, that's what I thought. I could be wrong."

"A small thing," said Benz-Fisher. "The First World War was fought over a small thing. A scrap of people. And twenty million men died. Mind you, they'd mostly have been dead by now anyway. I suppose there's some comfort in that." He was abstracted by his thoughts. He was seeing rows of little white crosses stretching away in diminishing perspective toward infinity. Terence shifted uncomfortably and said, "If you don't want me, I've got one or two things—"

"But I do want you. I want you to keep an eye on this lawyer in search of cheap publicity. Tony can help you. I want to know where he goes and who he sees. And we'll get a tap on his office line. No need to do it officially."

Terence said, "I suppose you know what you're up to."

"You suppose wrongly. I haven't the faintest idea what I'm up to. Do you know what to do if you're lost in a fog? Walk downhill. If you walk downhill far enough, you're bound to get to somewhere in the end. Even if it's only out to sea."

Terence said, "I'd better get on with it, eh?"

"I've had another thought."

Terence nearly said, "Oh, Gawd," but thought better of it. You could take liberties with B.F. when he was in a certain mood, but his moods changed very quickly.

"I wonder if this is a case where Mr. Stukely might be able to help us?"

"Could be."

"Do we know where he is?"

"It's a year or two now. He might be almost anywhere."

"That's true. He might be anywhere in the whole wide world. A tiny particle floating unseen on the boundless tide of humanity. A speck of protoplasm, a millionth of a millionth of an inch in diameter. A microcosm." Benz-Fisher returned to earth with a rush. He said, "All the same, I think he's somewhere in London. Let me have his last address."

After Terence had taken himself off, Benz-Fisher sat for a few moments staring at the closed door. He was wondering why he put up with Terence. A cheeky little sod, and totally insignificant. But that, of course, was his strength. He was so insignificant that no one ever noticed him, not until it was too late. Like a trypanosoma. The thought of Terence as a flagellate infusorian protozoan pleased him so much that he took up a pen and sketched the little creature on the margin of a top secret report he was reading. It had a rudimentary tail at one end and Terence's snub-nosed face at the other.

The buzzer on his desk sounded. The voice of Terence said, "We've only got this old address. It's a crummy sort of residential hotel. I gave them a ring, but they couldn't help. It was more than three years ago. You couldn't expect anything, really."

"I never expect anything," said Benz-Fisher. "That's why I'm never disappointed. I'm going out to have a bathe."

"Keep walking downhill," said Terence, "and you'll reach the sea." But he had taken the precaution of switching off the intercom before he said it.

On his way back from the R.A.C., where he had enjoyed an excellent bathe, Benz-Fisher called in at the steel and glass palace which is the new New Scotland Yard. Here he spent ten minutes with a detective superintendent in the Special Branch, spoke on the superintendent's own telephone to a detective sergeant at West End Central, and came away with the address that he wanted. It was a restaurant in Soho with pretensions to haute cuisine.

There was a small vestibule near the entrance for the hanging of hats and coats. As Benz-Fisher took off his light topcoat, the wallet in his breast pocket slipped out and slid down onto the carpeted floor. The headwaiter picked it up and was hurrying after its owner when his eye caught sight of the card which occupied the talc-covered slot which is normally reserved for a season ticket. The lighting in the vestibule was more efficient than in the body of the restaurant, and he was able to read what was printed on the card. A few moments later he was restoring the wallet to Benz-Fisher. Having handed him over to the attentions of a subordinate, he slid out of the room and into the little office at the far end.

"We have a visitor," he said.

The proprietor looked up from the wine merchant's catalogue he was studying and said, "What visitor?"

The headwaiter murmured the words.

"You're sure?"

"I happened to see his card."

"Have a word with the chef. And take his order yourself."

Benz-Fisher enjoyed a very tolerable meal, seasoned with a bottle of fifteen-year-old Chambertin, and followed by a cigar. No brandy. To drink brandy after good burgundy was a gastronomic tautology. It was nearly eleven o'clock when he called for his bill. The proprietor brought it himself.

"I hope you have enjoyed your meal, sir."

"I have enjoyed it very much," said Benz-Fisher, "and I shall say so."

"You will say so?" The proprietor's surprise was nicely done.

"I am here partly on pleasure, but partly on business too." He extracted, from the front of his wallet the card which had already excited the headwaiter and which identified Mr. Winstanley as an Inspector of the Gastronomic Guide of England and Wales. He presented it to the proprietor.

"Had we known," said the proprietor reverently, "we would have made a very special effort."

"I am sure you would," said Benz-Fisher. "That, of course, is why we never announce ourselves. But there *is* something you can do for me."

"Anything, Mr. Winstanley."

"I have been trying for some time to locate a man, a Mr. Stukely. He used to work for our organization. We would very much like to get in touch with him again."

"Stukely. No. I don't think . . ."

"You might not know his name, but I think you might recognize him if I described him. He is tallish, distinguished-looking, has gray hair, which he wears rather long and swept back. He has a small gray beard, of the type which used to be called an imperial. Also, he sometimes uses a monocle."

"Ah, yes. Certainly I have seen him here. But not recently."

"How recently?"

"Not for several months. Nevertheless, I may be able to help you. If it is the man I am thinking of, he was usually accompanied on his visits here by . . . a female." With a quick gesture, employing both hands, he sketched the outlines of an hour-glass figure.

"A female," agreed Benz-Fisher. "And let us not be too delicate about the matter—a female of a certain class."

"Yes. Indeed. Perhaps I make myself clear if I say that had she appeared alone I could not have admitted her."

"You could hardly make yourself clearer. And you think you can help me to locate her?"

"The gentleman referred to her by the name of Aileen. And unless she has changed her job in the last few weeks, you will find her at the Extravaganza in Barnaby Street. I should, however, warn monsieur that it is not quite the sort of establishment to which monsieur is accustomed."

"When on duty, one must go where duty calls." As he said this, Benz-Fisher smiled. The proprietor, a student of human nature, thought he had never seen a smile so genial, so meaningless, and so curiously disturbing. But Benz-Fisher was smiling because he was happy. The food had not been sensational, but the wine had been. A Chambertin was always a toss-up. A vineyard which was divided between eighteen owners could produce, under the same label, a wine which varied from ordinary to superb, and this had been very high up the scale. He guessed that it was not the wine of that name on the wine list but came from the proprietor's private cellar.

The entrance to the Club Extravaganza was a narrow doorway between a shop which sold books and magazines to the public and a shop which sold glassware to the trade. Over the door an illuminated sign said, "Non-Stop Strip-Tease. Double and Treble Acts. Sophisticated Fun." Rocking gently from his heels forward onto his toes and back again, Benz-Fisher studied the announcement with the care of an Egyptologist deciphering a cuneiform inscription. A sad-looking man in a hussar uniform studied Benz-Fisher with like care. Eventually he said, "Make your mind up, sir. Lovely girls. None of them over fifty."

"I appreciate the matronly figure."

"Lots of them inside. Ever so matronly."

Benz-Fisher completed one oscillation, came to rest, and said sharply, "You're not touting for business, are you?"

"Certainly not, sir. Just passing the time of day."

"Because you appreciate, I hope, that touting for business in the open street is contrary to London licensing regulations."

"I'm not in the street."

"No," said Benz-Fisher with sinister emphasis, "but *I* am."

"If you don't want to come in, sir—"

"I do. And I wish to see the proprietor."

"I'm afraid Mr. Carlotti isn't here just now."

"There must be someone in charge. If you don't produce him quickly, I shall fetch a policeman."

The doorman looked at him speculatively. He had stood outside this and similar doorways for a long time and prided himself that he could place any visitor at sight. The drunk, the bashful, the furtive, the plainclothes policeman, the social visitor, the newspaperman. But he had to confess that this one had him beat.

However, the first and the last rule was no fuss. He said, "Come this way, sir."

Halfway down the stairs was a small lighted landing. On the left of this landing was a door marked private. The doorman knocked and went inside, shutting it behind him. Benz-Fisher stood on the landing perfectly still with his head bent forward, listening.

From the curtained foot of the stairs came the sound of music, recorded and amplified. The curtains were pushed aside and a young man came out and ran up the steps. He saw Benz-Fisher at the last moment, managed to avoid bumping into him, and said, "It's a bloody swindle. The girls won't take off— Oh. Sorry. I thought you were the commissionaire."

"I'm a detective superintendent," said Benz-Fisher. "If you have a complaint to make—"

"It doesn't matter," muttered the young man. He ran up the second flight of stairs and out into the street. He seemed anxious to get into the open air.

The office door opened and the doorman looked out. He said, "The boss wants to know who you are."

"I'll tell him myself," said Benz-Fisher. It was difficult to see how he managed it, but one moment he was outside the office door, which was blocked by the doorman. The next moment he was inside.

The man standing behind the desk could have been no one else but Mr. Carlotti. He was a Mediterranean islander, Maltese or Sicilian. Advancing years and prosperity, which had added a layer of fat, could not conceal the broad shoulders and thick thighs of an athlete. He stared at Benz-Fisher, and Benz-Fisher stared back at him. It was a conflict of wills. Mr. Carlotti conceded a point by being the first to break the silence. He said, "Well, what is it?"

"You are Mr. Carlotti?"

"I believe so."

"Then I think we had better continue this conversation in private. In any event, your man had better get back on the door. While I was outside, three men came in without paying."

"No one pays at the door. This is a members' club."

"That was one of the things I wanted to find out," said Benz-Fisher. He took out a small book and made a note in it.

"What is all this?"

"I have come to inspect your premises."

"Inspect!"

"Pursuant to the powers vested in me by the licensing regulations for members' clubs issued by the Greater London Council. You have a copy?"

A shade of indecision showed for the first time on Mr. Carlotti's face. Benz-Fisher said, "Not only should you have a copy, but the rules in the First Schedule should be displayed on your premises."

Mr. Carlotti gestured to the commissionaire, who slid out of the room. He said, "You have some identification?"

"Certainly."

From his capacious wallet Benz-Fisher selected a card and handed it to Mr. Carlotti, who studied it carefully. He said, "This seems an odd hour for you to be making an inspection, Mr. Benskin."

Benz-Fisher swung around on him. His face had gone red, almost livid. "If you doubt my credentials," he blared, "telephone the police. West End Central. You know the number. Ask for Superintendent Falk."

It was like the door of a furnace swinging open to let out the stored-up heat within. Mr. Carlotti said, "I am not doubting your credentials, sir. I only said that inspections usually take place during the day."

"My inspections take place when I bloody well choose to make them. Now, if you'll be so good—"

"You wish to see the girls?"

"Sweat, tits, and five o'clock shadow. I'm not interested in your girls. I wish to see the lavatories, the washing accommodations, the changing rooms, and the fire precautions. I should particularly draw your attention to rules which were promulgated last year about the flameproofing of curtains."

"It is not always easy to do these things at once," said Mr. Carlotti. He sounded subdued. He led the way by a farther door and down a flight of stone steps. They were in the backstage area and the noise of the music and voices came to them faintly.

Benz-Fisher's inspection was minute. He measured the

changing rooms, pacing out the distances and entering them in his notebook. He tested the fire exit, which opened grudgingly. He even penetrated into the tiny lavatories.

"The girls are so careless," said Mr. Carlotti. "Constantly I instruct them—"

"Constantly they ignore your instructions," said Benz-Fisher and made a further note.

In the distance a bell rang. There was a thudding of feet, and half a dozen girls raced along the passage, burst into the room where the two men were standing, and started to change. Changing involved putting on clothes rather than taking them off. During this process they ignored Mr. Carlotti but were unable to take their eyes off the visitor. His bowler hat seemed to fascinate them.

Benz-Fisher, who had been examining them with equal interest, said, "Is one of you called Aileen?" The chattering stopped. A big blonde at the end of the line said, "Suppose it is."

Her body said twenty-five, but her face, in the unfriendly light of the changing room, said forty.

"If your name should happen to be Aileen," said Benz-Fisher with a winning smile, "I should like five minutes' conversation with you."

"We're on again in five minutes."

"That's all right," said Mr. Carlotti. "Go along and have a word with the gentleman. He won't eat you, you know."

"It wasn't eating I was worrying about," said Aileen.

"Hurry along with you. You can use the end room."

When they were alone, Benz-Fisher wasted no time. He said, "You've been seeing a lot of a man lately. I don't know what name he's using, but I'll describe him."

Aileen said, "O.K. I've been out with him once or twice. That's not a crime, is it?"

Benz-Fisher regarded her thoughtfully. Seen at close quarters and in undress, there was something overpowering about Aileen. Eat her? She would have made a meal for six hungry tigers. He visualized six tigers in a circle licking their lips, with Aileen in the middle.

He said, "It's not a crime to be seen about with a man who's wanted for questioning. But it might be an indiscretion."

"Questioning? Who *are* you, mister?"

Benz-Fisher produced a warrant card.

"A busy. I thought you were, the way Carlo was crawling round you. What do you want?"

"I want this man's address. And please don't pretend you don't know it."

"Suppose I don't want to tell you. That's not a crime either. Unless they've changed the law."

"If you won't tell me," said Benz-Fisher, "I shall close this place down. Which I have power to do. It's broken about six out of ten of the regulations. *And* I shall tell Mr. Carlotti why I'm closing it down, and whose fault it is. I don't think he'd be pleased."

"You're a proper sod, aren't you," said Aileen. She said it without rancor. "All right. He's calling himself Fairfax. Major Fairfax. And he's staying at the Claygate Hotel. It's behind Baron's Court Underground. At least, that's where he was last week. Don't blame me if he's moved on again."

"Who could possibly blame a beautiful girl like you," said Benz-Fisher.

Sometime after he had left the club, the doorman said to Mr. Carlotti, who was, in fact, his son-in-law, "Do you think he really was a whatever he said. An inspector?"

"No, I don't."

"Then why didn't you sling him out?"

"Because," said Mr. Carlotti, "he had authority of some sort behind him."

"What did he want with Aileen?"

"The address of one of her friends."

"I think we had better get rid of that girl."

"I have already done so," said Mr. Carlotti.

Cedric Lyon, the senior metropolitan magistrate at the West London Court, looked like an old-fashioned preparatory school headmaster, and he treated his mixed clientele of careless motorists, forgetful husbands, pugnacious drinkers, street traders, and prostitutes in much the same way that a headmaster would have done. A warning here, a hundred lines there; in extreme cases six of the best.

He was not a fool. He had read the papers and had recognized that this was something which could be important. Also he had noted that the press bench, which was usually occupied only by a young man from the *Chelsea and Kensington Clarion,* was now packed to suffocation with older and much more experienced-looking men. He had observed these portents and had determined not to be intimidated.

Having granted an extension of bail, a further adjournment of eight days in a petty larceny charge, and an interim order for the payment of five pounds a week to a deserted mother, he inquired of his clerk whether there were any further applications. The clerk looked carefully through his list and said, "One further application, your honor. Jonas Killey, appearing in person."

Jonas, who had been fidgeting with a large folder of papers, leaped to his feet. Mr. Lyon said, "One moment, if you don't mind," and to the police sergeant standing at the back of the court, "Would you mind opening the window, Sergeant. We shall have to tolerate a slight increase in noise in the interests of hygiene. I have informed the authorities more than once of the intolerable condition of this court in summer. We have the choice of being asphyxiated or deafened. Yes, Mr. Killey?"

Jonas said, raising his voice to combat the noise of passing traffic, "I would like to start by drawing your attention, your honor, to the history."

"That's all right, Mr. Killey. I've read the papers. Just make your application."

"I'm afraid that the early history of this matter is relevant. I shall have to deal with it."

"It's for me to say what is relevant and what is not relevant. You are applying to the court to issue a summons against William Frederick Dylan calling on him to answer criminal charges arising out of certain incidents alleged to have taken place more than eight years ago. Those are the only facts in the history of the matter which are relevant. Will you now produce the proofs in support of your application?"

"I protest most emphatically against this treatment. This is a court of law and I am entitled to be heard fully and fairly."

"Are you trying to teach me my duty, Mr. Killey?"

"If it proves necessary, I may have to do that."

For a moment, Mr. Lyon nearly let himself go. Then experience won a close victory. He saw the pencils of the reporters poised. He visualized the massed ranks of public opinion. He turned on a smile that was entirely artificial, but unexpectedly effective, and said, "Very well, Mr. Killey. I'm never too old to learn. You shall proceed at your own pace."

It would have been easier if the window had been shut, but Jonas did his best. He quoted passages from trade union regulations and extracts from the accounts of ACAT and MG. It took a long time, because Mr. Lyon made notes in longhand, and anything which coincided with the passage of a lorry or a motorcycle had to be repeated. It was midday before Jonas resumed his seat. For the last few minutes Mr. Lyon had not been taking notes. He had been considering, with great care, exactly what he was going to say.

He addressed the courtroom rather than Jonas, but he spoke as though he was well aware that his words were aimed at a much wider audience.

He said, "In this country, unlike many foreign countries, we have no state prosecuting system. And even the fact that we have seen fit to join the Economic Community of Europe"—Mr. Lyon bared his teeth in a grimace which demonstrated his views on the Common Market—"does not mean that we have adopted their judicial system. In this country the citizen is the prosecutor. In most cases the police shoulder the burden for him. In very serious cases the Director of Public Prosecutions may intervene. But the principle remains intact. Any member of the public who considers that a crime has been committed has the right and the duty to prosecute the criminal. I mention these facts to put this application into perspective. I think we'll have that window shut now."

Patrick Mauger, who was wedged between the *Express* and the *Guardian*, said, "The old man's being pretty cagey, isn't he?"

"He's going on record for posterity," said the *Express*.

"*And* the Court of Appeal," said the *Guardian*.

"However," said Mr. Lyon, "if such a system is to work satisfactorily, if the courts are not to be inundated with summonses, and innocent people are not to stand in daily peril of groundless accusations brought out of spite, certain precautions are necessary.

"The first, and most important of these is that the applicant should satisfy a magistrate that prima facie grounds exist for supposing that some crime has been committed. It is not neces-

61

sary for him to prove it. Proof will come later. But there must be shown to be solid grounds, backed by acceptable evidence. In this case Mr. Killey has based his application on two documents. The first is a photographic copy of a set of accounts of a defunct body called the Aluminium, Copper, and Allied Trades Union. He described the accounts as 'audited,' but this I find questionable. In my view accounts are not audited until they have been inspected and certified by a properly qualified accountant, which is apparently not the case here.

"The second document is an official copy of the annual return of an existing trade union, the Mining and General Metal Workers, who at that date absorbed the smaller union. There is, as Mr. Killey has pointed out, a discrepancy between these documents so far as the Provident Fund is concerned. There could be various explanations for this, the most likely, one might think, being that the unions would both incur expenses in a transaction of this sort. To this, Mr. Killey says no. He tells us that he was involved in the transaction and knows that no expense fell on the smaller union.

"I did not find this convincing. He has produced no documentary evidence in support of it except something which he described as a draft agreement; which I am quite unable to accept. Nor has he given any adequate explanation of why Mr. Dylan, the treasurer of the smaller union, who was on the point of changing to a much better paid and more important job with the larger union, should have been moved to put a relatively small sum of money in his own pocket. He suggested that Mr. Dylan might have been short of money at the time, but since he did not pursue the point, I think he realized that it was mere supposition. To sum the matter up, I find this application based on two documents, one of which, being an unauthenticated copy, would not be admitted in a court of law. I cannot find anything here which approaches prima facie evidence of a criminal act, and I shall not grant the application."

There was a moment of silence, and it was not clear whether

Mr. Lyon, who was still looking down at his notes, had finished or not. Then he raised his eyes, looked directly at Jonas Killey, and said, "I do not normally find it necessary to add any personal comment on matters which come before me, but in this case, in fairness to the person who has been named, I feel it incumbent on me to add that I think it is a pity that this application should ever have been made."

Jonas pushed through the crowd of reporters waiting outside the court, not rudely, but quite firmly, hailed a passing taxi, and was driven back to his office. He was not a sensitive man, but his cheek was still tingling from the slap administered by Mr. Lyon.

Willoughby met him in the outer office, saw from his face that matters had not gone well, and refrained from comment.

Jonas beckoned him into his own room and said, "I shall be going up to Sheffield on Monday. I shall probably be away for two days. It could even be three. Is there anything you can't handle?"

Together they examined the entries in Jonas' diary and decided that one client could be put off and the others coped with.

"There's only one thing," said Willoughby. "We're a bit short of cash in the office account."

"Cash for what?"

"The cleaners are a month adrift. I expect they'll wait. But the rates have got to be paid."

"How much?"

"Just over two hundred pounds. It was due in March, but we

held them off by raising that technical point over the assessment. They're not going to wait much longer."

"The bank will let us have it, won't they?"

"I hope so," said Willoughby. "The last time I ran into the manager, he dodged down a side street. I thought that was a bad sign."

Jonas was not really listening. His mind was far away. He was gathering supporting evidence, compiling a dossier, tracking down facts, subpoenaing witnesses. The senior judge in the Court of Appeal was saying, "Having listened to the convincing case put forward by the appellant, we have no hesitation . . ."

"Suppose they won't," said Willoughby.

"Won't what?"

"Suppose the bank won't let us overdraw any further."

"You'll have to do the best you can," said Jonas impatiently. "You young chaps have got no initiative. Ask Mrs. Warburton if she'd be good enough to bring her book in. I must clear up some of these letters before I go."

But when Mrs. Warburton appeared, she had no book. She said, "It's them again."

"What on earth are you talking about?"

"You remember those two men who came to see you yesterday. They're here again. Or one of them is."

"I can't see him."

"I'll tell him."

She was back in two minutes looking flustered.

"He won't go away."

"Really," said Jonas. "This is ridiculous. Well, if he won't go away, I suppose he'll just have to sit there. Now, to the Inspector of Taxes, Richmond District. You've got his address and reference. Dear Sir . . ."

The door opened a few inches and the pink face of Ben Thomas peered around it. "Terribly sorry to interrupt."

"*Will* you get out."

"Won't take a minute."

"If you don't get out, I shall be forced to summon assistance and have you thrown out."

The threat did not seem to worry Ben Thomas a lot. He looked like a man who had been thrown out of a lot of places. He said, "I was in court this morning. I heard what the beak said to you. I had an idea you weren't going to take it lying down."

"Indeed. Well, you happen to be right about that."

Ben insinuated himself farther into the room. He said, "If that's right, I had an idea that might help. Look, this won't take a second. But it's rather confidential."

Jonas hesitated and then said, "As long as it's quick. If you wouldn't mind, Mrs. Warburton."

Mrs. Warburton bristled, but she withdrew.

"I guess you'll be going up north to collect some of the bits and pieces that old virgin on the bench thought you ought to have. Mind you, I think he was being sticky for the hell of it."

"He wasn't exactly cooperative," said Jonas. It was refreshing to learn that someone else shared his opinion of Cedric Lyon, even if it was a vulgar little man wearing a made-up bow tie.

"What I thought was this. The sort of evidence you're looking for, if it's anywhere it's in Todmoor. And round the ASIA smelter. They're odd sort of people up there. What you might call close. They say the only thing a Yorkshireman will give you free is his opinion of you."

"I don't imagine it's going to be easy to find what I want, but I think I shall do it."

"Right," said Ben. "And that's where I might be able to help. Have you got a bit of paper? Then write down this name and address. Edgar Dyson, 109 Cowgate. That's in Framhill, outside Sheffield. Don't try ringing him up. Go round and see him, in the evening. He'll be expecting you. He's usually home by six, but give him time to have his tea first. Got it?"

As Ben moved to the door, Jonas said, "Yes. But look here.

You haven't told me anything about him. Who is he? How do I know he'll see me?"

"He's convener of the shop stewards at ASIA," said Ben. "He'll see you."

Benz-Fisher did not himself attend at the West London Magistrates Court. He sent Terence along instead. It was his policy to appear very little in public and he was particularly careful to avoid places where he might encounter old acquaintances from the bar. Also, he had work to do.

At twelve o'clock, at the moment when Mr. Cedric Lyon was gathering up his notes preparatory to giving judgment, Benz-Fisher was walking down Loftus Road, which is a street of small hotels, guest houses, and boarding houses behind Baron's Court Underground Station. As he ambled along the pavement in the hot sunshine, he pondered over a nice semantic problem. When does a hotel become a guest house? When does a guest house become a boardinghouse? It was a question as full of subtleties and distinctions as the English class system.

"It's a matter of degree," he decided.

"I beg your pardon," said a scholarly-looking old man who was passing him at that moment.

"I said, what delightful weather we were having."

"I'm not deaf," said the old man. "You said something about degrees."

"Eighty-two degrees Fahrenheit according to the papers."

The old man looked at him suspiciously, clacked a fine set of false teeth, and went on his way. Benz-Fisher climbed the well-whitened steps of the Claygate Family and Commercial Hotel.

In the red and black tiled hall a colored photograph of Queen Mary encased in pearls beamed down on a healthy-looking rubber plant in a brass pot. To the right of the rubber plant was the reception desk. Behind the reception desk sat a woman with something of Queen Mary's marmoreal dignity.

She inclined her head toward Benz-Fisher, who bowed fractionally in return, produced a card from his wallet, and said, "The syndicate sent me along."

"The syndicate?"

"The syndicate who own this hotel. And most of the others round here, I gather."

"Oh, them."

"As you will see, madam, it is my job to check on bad payers."

The manageress studied the card which had been placed on the desk in front of her. It stated that Arthur F. Mapledurham was an agent of the Hotel Protection and Credit Managers Association.

"We have a very faithful clientele," said the manageress. "Many of them stay with us for months. Some of them even longer. One of my oldest clients, a Mrs. Margesson, was buried from here only last Thursday. She had been with us for seven years."

"Faithful even unto death," said Benz-Fisher. The thought appeared to affect him. He removed his bowler hat. "There was one of your guests I was told to look out for. We have him on our books from another occasion. A Major Fairfax."

"Ah. Yes. A very pleasant gentleman. We *have* had a little trouble with him. Nothing serious."

"How up to date is he?"

The manageress went through the motions of consulting a ledger on the desk in front of her, but it was clear that she knew the answer.

"He's a bit behind," she agreed.

"How many weeks?"

"I am afraid it's five weeks. Including this week, that is. Accounts are settled on Friday."

"And this one has not been settled for five Fridays? Do you usually allow your guests to run up bills of this size?"

"I spoke to the major about it only last Monday. He told me

that he was expecting a dividend from his family company. It makes motor mowers."

"It will have to be a very large dividend to pay this bill. Five weeks at twenty-four pounds a week. That's a hundred and twenty pounds. Add the extras. Now what can they be? Mostly drink, I fear."

"The major likes a drink from time to time. He never takes more than is good for him though."

"His excesses are, I am sure, financial rather than alcoholic." Benz-Fisher was adding up the figures as he spoke. "I make it £184. That's a very large sum of money to be outstanding, is it not?"

"It's a large sum. But I feel certain he'll pay it."

"Optimism is a virtue. But it must not be carried to excess. We must beware of the Micawber that lurks in all of us."

"I don't think he's got anything like that."

"Let it pass," said Benz-Fisher. "I will have a word with the major. Is he in the hotel?"

"He's in the lounge. You could see him in my office. I wouldn't want any fuss. Most of our guests are elderly and easily upset."

"The H.P.C.M.A. is *not* the Gestapo, madam. We employ persuasion, not force."

When Major Fairfax was shown into the office, Benz-Fisher had stationed himself on the hearth rug, with his hands behind his back and his head thrust forward, as though he was about to charge. It was a stance he had copied from his housemaster at Marlborough. The major, receiving the full impact of his personality, appeared for a moment to be contemplating flight. Then he came forward, held out a hand, and said, "This is a surprise. Mr. Acworth, isn't it?"

Benz-Fisher ignored the outstretched hand. He rose slightly onto his toes and said, "In trouble again?"

"I'm afraid I don't understand."

"Running into debt again. Where's the money coming from? And don't talk to me about dividends."

"It's true that I am somewhat in arrears—"

"Two hundred pounds."

"Is it as much as that? Oh, dear. Everything is so expensive these days."

"You're an improvident old person. If you don't mend your ways, you'll end up in bankruptcy and disgrace. By pure chance, however, a further matter has turned up in which you may be able to assist me. So sit down and pay attention. First I am going to give you some names and addresses. You can write them down, but when you have learnt them, you will destroy the paper. You had better use your legal name. Stukely. Reginald Owen Stukely."

"You think that's wise?"

"It may not be wise, but it's necessary. If you were called upon to give evidence, it might cast some doubt on your bona fides, don't you think, if the opposition discovered that you were using a—what shall I call it, Major?—a *nom de guerre.*"

"I suppose so," said the major.

"Very well. Pay attention. There is a solicitor with offices in Wimbledon. Yes, write this down too, but check him up in the Law List. I think it's a one-way firm, but if there's a salaried partner you'd better find out about him too."

"Since you speak of proceedings, do I take it that we are contemplating a Herman operation?"

"That is correct. I shall be paying you six hundred pounds. With it you will first discharge all your liabilities here. In fact, I will do that for you. I shall explain that the Association is lending you the money, secured on your dividends. You receive dividends from time to time, I understand."

"Quite unexpected ones sometimes," agreed the major happily.

"Very well. The next hundred pounds you will spend on equipping yourself. Your suit, though respectable, has been cleaned and pressed too often for the role I have in mind. There is no time to have one made. Go to Austin Reed's. They have a wide selection of ready-made suits. Shirts, shoes, an umbrella, a brief case. I leave the details to you. And you will need a haircut. There are only three barbers in London who cut hair properly. Go to Truscott's. If you say that I sent you—here's my card—they'll fit you in somehow."

The major pocketed the card, noting without apparent surprise that it bore the name of a well-known northern landowner and race-horse breeder.

"The balance of the six hundred pounds is for you. I shall also be entrusting you with a further large sum of money. I sincerely hope that you will not be tempted to divert any of it to your own use. The last man who attempted such an indiscretion is in Bedingfield Criminal Lunatic Asylum. He tells the doctors, when they visit him from time to time, that he was framed by the Secret Service. He assures them of it with tears in his eyes. The specialists have an extensive file on him. They regard him as an interesting case of compulsive delusion."

For a moment the major seemed to have some difficulty in speaking. In the end he said, "You can rely on me."

"I'm sure I can," said Benz-Fisher.

When he got back to the office he found Terence waiting for him. "Well," he said. "How did it go?"

"Application refused."

"Excellent."

"I'm not sure."

"And what do you mean by that?"

"If the beak had handled him properly, it might have been all right. I don't say it would have been, because Killey's an obstinate bugger if ever I saw one."

"And Mr. Lyon didn't handle him with tact."

"Tact!" said Terence. "If he'd brought out a hammer and hit him over the head with it, that would have been more tactful. He started by trying to bully him. When he saw that wouldn't work, he sat back licking his lips and waiting his turn. Everyone in court except Killey could see what was coming. Then he delivered a short sermon on the sanctity of the British legal system, refused the application, and gave him a parting kick in the pants. The press wasn't interested in the sermon, but they wrote that last bit down word for word. You'll see it in all the papers tomorrow."

"Did he step out of line far enough for an appeal on the grounds of prejudice?"

"I'm not a lawyer," said Terence, "but the idea did cross my mind. I've a feeling it occurred to Killey too."

Benz-Fisher said, "That's a pity." In moments of real crisis he practiced a studied moderation of language. "A lot will depend on how the newspapers treat it. There'll be something in the later editions of the evening papers, but the real crunch will come tomorrow morning."

"That was another thing I noticed," said Terence. "The men who were there weren't the ordinary court reporters. The *Express* and the *Telegraph* had their top political men there. And the *Watchman* had sent—what's his name? The chap who's doing a profile on Will Dylan."

"Patrick Mauger."

"That's the chap. He was lapping it all up. He looked just the sort of bright-eyed young bastard who'd jump on any bandwagon that was going."

"No doubt," said Benz-Fisher. "But the question is, *Which way is this bandwagon going?*"

Edward Lambard signed the last of the forty letters on his desk, got his car out of the garage behind the Prudential where it lived during the week, and drove home to his house at Shere. The road south was achock with the coast-going traffic, but at Dorking he was able to shake himself clear. He swung the big Bentley up the hill onto the Godalming Road, passing the clock at Abinger Hammer at the exact moment that the man was coming out to hit the bell for seven o'clock. He would be home in good time for a bath and a drink before eating. He hoped that his wife had not invited anyone to dinner.

There was a Reliant Scimitar in the drive, which he recognized. A battered Volkswagen would have indicated his daughter Penelope. The Scimitar meant that his son Jonathan had wangled some leave and was planning to honor them with his presence for the night. He would not waste a whole weekend on them. The girl he was currently pursuing, with intentions which were entirely dishonorable, lived near Brighton, and he would doubtless be on the trail early next morning.

Mr. Lambard felt that Jonathan would be easier to take after he had had his bath. He ran the car quietly into the garage, went through the connecting door into the house, and made his way unobserved to his own bedroom.

Half an hour later, the grime of London washed away and the dark gray uniform of London discarded in favor of a suit of ancient brown tweed, he came downstairs. As he approached the drawing-room door, he heard Jonathan's voice, high-pitched, clipped, and intolerant.

Someone, he gathered, as he opened the door, had been making trouble.

"Ah, there you are," said his wife. "I thought I heard you come in. Pour your father a drink, Jonathan."

Jonathan moved his long corduroy-covered legs languidly across the room.

"Whisky," said Lambard, "and don't be stingy with it. Who's been making trouble?"

"Chap called Killey. Didn't you see it? It was splashed in the evening papers."

"I might have done, if I could read a paper while I was driving a car. Not too much water."

"You used to know him, didn't you, darling? He was in your firm."

"Certainly I knew him. Tom Buller was talking about him the

other day. He's not a bad chap, but he's got a bee in his bonnet."

"The man is a menace," said Jonathan. He said it in exactly the same conclusive and unappealable tone that his colonel would have used standing in front of the ante-room fire.

"Surely he's not threatening the Blues," said his father.

"He's not big enough to threaten anyone. He's an appalling little squirt, and he's engaging in the only sport that he and his sort understand. Mud slinging. In the ordinary way, it wouldn't matter, but he happens to be slinging it at a rather important man."

"I didn't know you studied politics, Jonathan."

"I know, I know. You think we're a lot of morons who do nothing but natter about horses and girls. But you're out of date. We've got a very intelligent crowd in the mess. Some of them would surprise you. Tim Lacey is as red as they come. Practically a card-carrying Communist. We used to pull his leg about it. Of course, he had to give it up when his uncle died and his father came into the title."

Lambard looked at him out of the corner of his eye to see whether Jonathan was joking and decided that he wasn't. It was an art which fathers acquire.

He said, "Are we waiting dinner for Penny?"

"She's not coming down," said his wife. "She telephoned this afternoon. She's standing in for someone at the hospital. It's too bad. She only gets one weekend off in four."

"Time she married some decent chap and settled down," said Jonathan. "And time we had dinner too. I'm going to bed early. Busy day tomorrow."

"Girl chasing, I suppose," said his father.

"Nothing of the sort," said Jonathan with dignity. "I'm playing polo at Cowdrey Park."

Other people were dismounting from their camels, pitching tents, spreading rugs, and preparing for two days of relaxation at the oasis of the British weekend.

Jonas joined old Mrs. Killey in her flat in Hornsey. Young Willoughby went home to Twickenham, where his father told him for the umpteenth time to get out and join a decent firm with prospects. Laurence Fairbrass spent the Saturday at Lord's, and Air Vice-Marshal Pulleyne disappeared altogether. Simon Benz-Fisher caught an early morning flight from Heathrow and was met at Nice airport by a blond woman in her early thirties, driving an Aston-Martin coupé. Mr. Stukely spent a very pleasant day shopping and had his hair cut by Mr. Truscott in person. Patrick Mauger shut himself away in his flat and hammered out no less than three drafts of his profile on Will Dylan. It seemed to come out differently each time. Will took his family up river to Laleham in a motor cruiser, hired a skiff, and tried to teach Paul and Fred how to row. They all got very wet.

Christopher lay in a deck chair in his garden and watched his wife trying to teach Toby how to walk, an effort which was crowned with no success at all.

That was the end of the first week.

"I'll be plain with you," said Arnold Markstein. "I wish you hadn't come."

"I'm not asking for help," said Jonas stiffly. "Only for information."

"You're asking for trouble," said Markstein. He was barely five feet high, and a slight deformity of his neck and shoulders threw his head forward and gave him a gnomelike appearance. (Not one of those cheerful gnomes in red caps who preside over suburban lawns. A hard gnome, from the wilds of Edale Moor, from the caves and mines of Blackdean Edge and Crookstone Knoll.)

"If I'd had an ounce of sense, I'd have refused to see you. But you worked for me for five years. Did some good work too, till you got too big for your boots. I owe you something for that."

"I'd prefer our relationship to be on a business footing, and I'll pay—"

"You'll pay nothing. You don't seem to understand me. I know what you're up to. We read it all in the papers over the weekend. I'm against you. If there's any information I *have* to give you—anything which you could get out of me on discovery if you saw fit to litigate—then you shall have it." He took note of Jonas' reaction to this, and a very slight smile lifted the corner of his lip. He said, "You've been down south too long, boy. Up here we say what we mean and say it first time."

"I'll tell you what I'm looking for," said Jonas slowly. "If you've read an account of last Friday's proceedings, it must be obvious. I could only produce a photocopy of the last ACAT accounts and a made-up draft of the amalgamation agreement."

"Both stolen from this office when you left."

"If you care to put it that way."

"It's the truth. And I'll repeat it in open court if I have to. The judge won't be happy, I'd guess, about accepting two bits of paper which are secondhand *and* stolen."

"So you admit you've got the originals of both documents?"

"Certainly I admit it. How do you think you're going to get hold of them?"

"If those documents are vital to my case, there must be some process—"

"You're talking like a baby. My client is MG. If you were thinking of bringing a case against them, you might be able to force me to produce them. But you're not, are you?"

Jonas shook his head. He couldn't trust himself to speak.

"Your case, if it's a case at all, which I doubt, is against Dylan. He hasn't got these documents. And his solicitor won't have them either. So how are you going to force them to produce them?"

There was a long silence. At the end of it Markstein said, "You always were an awkward bugger. In some ways I respected you for it. A bit of what we call 'okkerdness' can be useful in our job. But like every virtue, it turns into a vice when you carry it too far."

Jonas was looking down at the floor. He still said nothing.

"Another thing, what do you think's happening to your practice while you're gallivanting about up north. It's hard enough to keep a practice going when you give your whole mind to the job. What are your partners going to say?"

"I haven't got any full partners, actually."

"Worse still. Who've you left in charge of the shop? The office boy?"

"I have a very capable salaried man."

There was another silence. Markstein looked at Jonas. He saw a white face, a set mouth, a tight jaw. He sighed and said, "Is there anything else you want to know?"

Jonas looked at a piece of paper he had taken out of his pocket. He said, "It would save me a bit of time if you could give me the present address of Raybould, Pentridge, and Barming."

"Those being the last trustees of ACAT before it got taken over."

"Correct."

"Raybould is dead, and Pentridge is in Canada."

"And Barming?"

"Sam Barming," said Markstein thoughtfully. "I believe he lives out at Todmoor, near the ASIA works. He retired last year. I expect people out there will be able to give you his address."

"Thank you. And Mr. Mason?"

"You were thinking of seeing him?"

"Yes."

"He's a very old man."

"But he's still alive?"

"Aye. He's still alive. He lives on Thorpe Common. The quickest way to get there is up the M.1. to the second Rotherham exit point. It's about half a mile back, on the right, down a side road. I'm not sure how you'd get there without a car."

"I'm hiring a car tomorrow morning. I shall need one in any event if I'm going out to Todmoor."

Markstein stared at him. He said, "They can read, you know."

"I don't follow you."

"The people at Todmoor. They've all read the papers too."

"I expect they have," said Jonas. He got up. As he turned to go, Markstein, who had been consulting a black indexed book on his tidy desk, said, "Mason's telephone number is Ecclesfield

0929. I should give him a ring before you go out there. Have a word with his sister. She looks after him."

"Thank you," said Jonas politely.

When he had gone, Markstein sat hunched in his chair, unmoving, for nearly a minute. Then he put out a hand, turned back the leaves of the book from M to B, picked up the telephone, and asked for a number.

The commercial hotel near the station served the meal which they described as tea at half past six. After Jonas had eaten it, he went out into the street.

When he had arrived at midday, Sheffield had been an oven, baking under the sun of that exceptional summer. Now a little coolness had come into the day. Jonas made his way to the bus terminus and boarded a bus for Owlerton and Framhill.

The rush hour was over, and the old Corporation two-decker trundled him along, first west, then north through nearly empty streets. As they approached Walkley, Jonas realized that he would pass the end of the street in which he had once lodged. It awoke no feelings of nostalgia. He was not a man who lived in the past.

By the time he had reached Framhill and found the street called Cowgate, the sun was going down in red glory, mellowing even that unromantic row of terrace houses. There was a small brass knocker on the front door of 109. Jonas tapped with it once or twice, unhopefully, and then banged with his knuckles on the glass. A voice shouted, "Oo is it? Come round the back."

He pushed open the gate which blocked the mouth of the tunnel between 109 and 111 and picked his way through an entanglement of deck chairs, prams, cartons, beer-bottle crates, and what looked like a small flying saucer. As he came out at the end, something white and soft hit him in the face.

"That's just Flossie being friendly," said a big man in shirtsleeves. He stretched out a hand and gathered up the white fantail pigeon from the back of a bench. "I thought I heard you knocking. I don't open that front door for anyone except the Queen, and she doesn't come here often."

He gave a great guffaw, and the neat white bird in his hand tilted its head and looked at him out of one eye.

"Time you were in bed," said the man. He flipped his wrist and the pigeon, seeming to understand him, volplaned across to the rambling tenement of boxes, sticks, and wire netting which filled the bottom of the garden.

"People'll tell you you can't keep fantails and racers together. They say they'll fight. It's a load of old knackers. I've been doing it for years. I'm Edgar Dyson."

"Pleased to meet you," said Jonas. "My name's Killey."

"They told me you might be around. Come inside and have a glass of beer. If you don't mind sitting in the kitchen."

"I may talk like a southerner," said Jonas. "But I was born in Lincolnshire and brought up in Sheffield."

"You're a lawyer," said Dyson. "You used to work for Markstein. Right?"

"That's right."

"We read about you in t'paper. The magistrate gave you a bloody nose. Now you've come up here to prove him wrong. Bide a moment and I'll get two glasses. The old woman's at bingo tonight, and we'll have to look after ourselves."

If Dyson wished to pose as a simple householder living in a back street, this was his business. The bluff speech, the kitchen, and the shirtsleeves did not deceive Killey for a moment. He had lived in the north. He recognized that he was in the presence of an unusual man. You were not elected convener in a factory employing four or five thousand men because you kept racing pigeons and slapped people on the back. The row of books which he saw on the shelf above the kitchen table wore the serviceable brown uniform of the Everyman Edition and had a well-thumbed look about them. Philosophers, economists, political scientists, thinkers, and dreamers. Marx rubbing shoulders with Hume and Mill.

Dyson returned with the beer. He said, "I got the word from friends down south. Anything I can do, in reason, I'll do it. But I warn you, you're swimming against tide. Cheers!"

"Tides turn."

"As long as you don't get drowned while you're waiting for 'em to do it." Dyson took a long pull at his beer, belched comfortably, and loosened his leather belt a couple of notches. "What have you come up here to find?"

"Two bits of paper. And one or two facts." He explained what he wanted. Dyson drank more beer and thought about it. He said, "When ACAT was on its own, things were done informal like. Not being a registered union, we made up a lot of our own rules. And we kept 'em when we felt like it. Times we didn't bother. Will Dylan was gaffer. The trustees did what he told 'em was best to do."

"But he had to produce accounts. And the trustees had to approve them."

"The trustees signed where he put his finger. Phil Raybould was an old woman. Matthew Pentridge was little more than a boy. He married a Canadian girl and went back to Canada with her, did you know?"

"Markstein told me."

"Sam Barming, he's different. Sam had a mind of his own. And a tongue." Dyson chuckled at some memory. "But he backed Will all the way. He'd seen him come up by the hard road, and he was like a father to him. More than a father. Fathers are quick enough to belt their sons. In Sam's eyes, Will could do no wrong. Mind you, I'm not saying he wasn't right about that. Will's a remarkable lad."

He refilled his own glass and topped up Killey's. "Your best chance of getting a signed set of accounts is from old Mason. If he hasn't lost 'em. As for the amalgamation agreement, MG have got a copy, no doubt. I'll see if I can get hold of it. 'Twon't be easy. The information you want. I'll put out a few feelers. If proceedings were started, there'll be some sort of record."

"It's very kind of you," said Jonas. "Tell me something. Why are you doing this for me?"

Dyson looked at him speculatively over the rim of his beer glass. He said, "As far as I'm concerned, the answer's easy. I'm doing it because I've been told to do it. It's you I'm wondering about. You're on the road to collect a lot of kicks and no ha'-pence. What's driving *you?*"

There were a lot of answers to this. Easy answers, which he had often given to himself. That it was intolerable that a crime should be committed and the criminal escape punishment because he was important or popular. That since he was the only man with all the requisite knowledge, it was clearly his duty to pursue the matter. And there were less comfortable answers. Answers in which pride and pique played their part. Under Dyson's candid gaze all of these answers seemed inadequate. In the end Jonas simply said, "If I didn't finish this thing off, I shouldn't think much of myself."

"Speaking as a man who likes peace and quiet," said Dyson, "I'm glad I've not got your conscience, lad. Drink up."

It was quite dark when Jonas went out into the garden. From the feathered tenement at the far end he could hear the rustling and clicking as the birds settled down for the night. The air was heavy with the scent of stocks and wallflowers and roses.

Dyson held a torch for him to help him through the dark passageway. As he went past he kicked the flying saucer. "My son made that," he said. "He thought he was going to fly to the moon in it."

Jonas walked slowly back to the bus stop. He had a lot to think about. Dyson's position in the matter was now fairly clear. He must be a member of the Communist Party, possibly of its extreme activist wing, the most disciplined of all the party organizations in the land. He was helping because he had been ordered to help, because presumably his masters had seen a political advantage in the upsetting of Dylan.

But there was more than that on his mind. The perversity of his nature was such that opposition stimulated him. The hostility of a man like Markstein had been a positive shot in the arm. Obstruction, enmity, polite disregard, apathy, were familiar dragons in his path. What he had found disconcerting was Dyson's friendliness.

If Dyson had been a different sort of man, his friendliness could have been discounted as mere softness. But he was clearly a fighter. A man who had carved out a small secure kingdom for himself and was now at ease in it.

At this point the bus arrived, and with it the first heavy drop of rain from the thunderclouds which had been rolling down since dusk from Snailsden Moss and Broomhead Moor.

The thunderstorm cracked and rumbled over Sheffield during the night but failed to clear the air. The false bright sunshine of the following morning held a threat of more to follow.

Jonas collected his car from the garage near the hotel and took the Rotherham road. At Motorway Junction 35 he turned right and, in a mile, right again. He was now in a country lane, running between fields on one side and a golf course on the other. A boy on a bicycle directed him to the Mason house. It was at the far side of the green and had its name, "Brenjam," on a shingle by the gate.

A female face at the window watched him as he walked up the red brick path, and a female person opened the door to him before he could touch the wrought-iron bell pull. She had a crop of iron-gray hair drawn back in a bunch over her skull, a powerful nose, and a mouth like the slot of a letterbox. She said, "You are Mr. Killey. I am Miss Mason. Come in."

"Who is it, Brenda?"

She marched to the door and said in the clearly enunciated tones that one uses when speaking to a child or a deaf person, "This is Mr. Killey, James. He telephoned from Sheffield. He has come to see you on business."

"Business, business," said Mr. Mason. He was perched in a high-backed padded chair near the window, with a rug tucked around his legs. Such hair as he still possessed was white, and his cheeks held that pink bloom which means health in youth and high blood pressure in old age.

"Come in, Mr. Killey. I'm afraid I can't get up. My legs aren't what they were."

"Please don't bother."

"It's very good of you to come all this way to see me. I can't quite recall what you wished to talk about, but if we can help you, we shall be glad to do so. When I say 'we' I mean my sister and myself. You won't mind my sister sitting in on our talk. She looks after all my affairs nowadays."

Jonas did mind. To deal with the artless Mr. Mason was one thing. His grenadier of a sister was a different proposition. He said, "What I had to say *was* rather confidential."

"Splendid," said Mr. Mason. "Then my sister will be just the person to deal with it."

Jonas turned to Miss Mason, who regarded him sardonically but said nothing. Jonas said, "Oh, very well. It's a little complicated, but I'll try to explain it."

He repeated what he had said to Markstein. At each pause in his exposition he received a smile and an encouraging bob from the white head opposite. When he had finished, Mr. Mason said, "I'm not very quick at grasping these matters, but Brenda will have understood it. She has a wonderful grip of business. Perhaps you could explain it to me, my dear?"

"Mr. Killey wants a copy of the last set of accounts you audited for ACAT."

"Oh?"

"But you can't find it, can you?"

"No."

"You looked for it, but you couldn't find it."

"I'm afraid that's right," said Mr. Mason, turning his pink placid face toward Jonas. "I'm very much afraid that's right. We both searched thoroughly, but we couldn't find what you wanted."

Jonas felt certain that the old man was lying. Markstein had warned them that he was coming and had told them what he wanted. The accounts were there. Accountants always kept one set for themselves. It was not all that long ago. If only he could get rid of the woman.

He said, "There's one other matter I have to discuss with Mr. Mason. It really is entirely confidential. Do you think I could speak to him alone for a moment?"

"No," said Miss Mason. She said it neither rudely nor abruptly, but in the firm and final tone in which a nurse refuses a child a treat. Jonas stared at her.

After a moment she said, "My brother doesn't care to see people alone. It worries him too much."

"That's right," said Mr. Mason. "I get worried."

He didn't look worried. He had traveled beyond the land of worry. He had crossed the frontier, into the land of illusion, and was heading for the land of sleep.

Miss Mason said, "Well, what is it?"

Jonas felt disinclined for further invention. He got up and said, "If I'm not permitted to speak to Mr. Mason in private, there's nothing more I can usefully say."

"That's that then," said Miss Mason. She also got up. Mr. Mason waved a white blue-veined hand toward him and said, "Good-bye, good-bye. I'm sorry you should have come so far to no good purpose. You'll have to excuse me not getting up. My legs aren't what they were."

When Jonas had gone, Miss Mason went into the room at the back of the house which was still referred to as the business room although no business had been done in it for many years. She unlocked a wooden cabinet, took out a green-covered set of accounts, and looked them over curiously. She wondered what secrets they contained which were important enough to bring a busy man all the way from London to look at them. They meant nothing to her, but Mr. Markstein's instructions had been quite clear. It was through Mr. Markstein that their pension check from ASIA reached them each month.

She put them back and relocked the cabinet.

Jonas was driving rather faster than he usually did, to exorcise his frustration. It took him half an hour to clear the northward sprawl of Sheffield, but as soon as he had passed through Sandygate he was in a different country. The road followed the course of the Rivelin stream, climbing steadily through Hollow Meadows and past Moscar Cross, where a board marked the extreme western limit of Yorkshire, and then dropping sharply to the Ladybower Reservoir.

It was a gaunt and somber landscape. In place of the soft limestone of the south, sharp peaks of millstone grit, tors, and edges slashed by sudden ravines crisscrossed lines of dry-stone wall, broken by patches of dark green grass where flowers seemed unwilling to grow.

As Jonas drove, the thought crossed his mind that in all the five or six years that he had lived and worked in Sheffield he had never suspected that this rugged savagery lay less than an hour's easy drive behind his back door. He had been too busy to waste his time admiring scenery. Now, for the first time, he felt something of its menace. The sun was still shining, but its light was hard and heavy. Behind the whaleback of Kinder Low and Edale Head a storm was building up.

From Ladybower Inn the road climbed south, skirting Bamford Edge, crossed the main railway line, and joined the main road to Todmoor and Castleton. Instead of following it into Todmoor, he turned aside directly up a minor road into the hills above. It was as though he wanted to spy out the land before venturing too far into it.

ASIA was spread out below him like a diagram in a primer of industrial geography. The quadruple line of pot rooms anchored to their own power station. The anode plant and cast house. The private line of rail which branched from the main line at the exit of the long Cowburn tunnel and brought the truckloads of raw alumina from Stretford Docks to the factory; and, striding away to the northeast, the double line of pylons which climbed over Win Hill and dipped down out of sight toward Ladybower.

The effect on Jonas was curious. He was seeing for the first time in the flesh something which had up to that point only been a symbol. He had read the name ASIA so many times, had written about it, thought about it, and argued about it; and here it was, suddenly spread out before him in hard outline. It was like going out one morning, turning a corner, and coming face to face with a well-known character out of a book.

He turned his car carefully and drove down to Todmoor.

A lady directed him to Sam Barming's house, which turned out to be a bungalow lying a few yards back from the main road and close to the works entrance to the smelter. Like the sailor who could not bear to be out of sight of the sea, Sam Barming had evidently decided to enjoy his retirement within sight and sound of his life's work.

As Jonas walked up the front path, the clouds finally overcame the sun and a shadow swooped down on the valley from Edale Moor. He rang the bell.

For a long minute nothing happened. Then he heard the thump of footsteps approaching, the door was flung open, and Sam Barming appeared. He was a big well-made man who had gone to seed, a human edifice in which almost everything was tumbling into ruin, dropped cheeks and chin, fallen shoulders, sagging stomach. He walked with the aid of a heavy rubber-tipped stick.

He said, "Well? Who is it? What do you want?"

Jonas said, "Can I come in?"

"Is that your car?"

"It's one I've hired."

"What did you say your name was?"

"I didn't. But it's Killey."

"It's what?"

"Killey."

"What do you want?"

"I'd like a word with you."

Mr. Barming seemed to be turning this over in his mind. Jonas saw his lips moving and the tip of his tongue appearing and disappearing like a snake looking cautiously out of its hole. Then he said, "Orright."

"Hadn't we better go inside?"

Mr. Barming turned and stumped away down the passage and into the living room, leaving Jonas to follow. It was a room which might have been neat and cheerful when Mrs. Barming was alive to look after it, but like its owner it had gone to seed.

Mr. Barming perched his sagging bottom on the corner of the table. Jonas chose one of the hard chairs beside it. They seemed to him to be safer than the cavernous armchairs in front of the fire. Mr. Barming swung one of his great legs slowly and said nothing. Jonas said, "I expect you know why I've come. I imagine that Markstein will have telephoned you."

Mr. Barming nodded and continued to say nothing.

"Then I won't waste a lot of your time."

Five minutes or five hours, it made no difference to Mr. Barming. He had the rest of his life to waste.

"What I'm looking for is a copy of the last set of accounts Dylan prepared for you. The final account before the amalgamation. You were one of the three trustees. I think you'll agree that it's your duty as a trustee to see that nothing went amiss with the funds of your union. After all, that's what you were elected for, isn't it?"

The darkening of Sam Barming's face was as ominous as the darkening of the landscape outside. Had Jonas been in any degree a sensitive man, he would have got up and got out—out of the house, out of Todmoor. Being Jonas, he settled more comfortably in his chair and prepared to improve the occasion.

He said, "If you consider the matter rationally, you will see that you have nothing to lose and everything to gain by cooperating with us. Consider the alternatives. If the discrepancy in the accounts can be cleared up, well and good. You'll have done Dylan a good turn, won't you? If, on the other hand, it should eventually transpire that he had been helping himself to union money, then your mates at the smelter will be thankful to you for seeing . . ."

Barming had levered himself off the edge of the table and was advancing on Jonas.

". . . for seeing that justice is done," concluded Jonas defiantly.

Sam Barming said, "You b-bastard. You f-f-fucking bastard." He was beyond anger. He was at the boiling point of rage where words shot out tripping over each other, bile and spittle mixed. "Coming here, asking me—me, Sam Barming—to help *you*. You—you've got a f-f-fucking nerve."

Jonas had got up too. He was not a coward, but there was something appalling about the bubbling fury of this wreck of what had once been a fine man.

"You're a lump, a lump of shit. You've never done a real day's work in your life, have you? Have you? Go on. Tell me. The only time you get your hands dirty is when you wipe your arse. Talking to me about my duty, my mates. You make me sick. Get out. Get out." He jabbed with his stick on the floor as Jonas backed away. "If I had that paper you want, if you offered me a million pounds for it, I'd burn it in front of your bloody eyes, mate."

Jonas was in the hall by now. Barming did not follow him. He started to laugh, and the laugh was more unnerving than the storm which had gone before.

The front door was still open. As Jonas went out, he noticed the men. There were a dozen of them, standing around his car.

He walked slowly down the path, fumbling for the car keys in his pocket with a hand which he tried to keep from shaking. Out of the corner of his eye he could see Barming standing at the window of the sitting room watching him. The men made no move. Like Barming, they seemed to be waiting on events.

There was something wrong with the car. It took Jonas a few seconds to realize what it was. Then he saw that all the tires were flat.

Jonas stared at them. One of the men laughed. Jonas whirled around and said, "Did you do this?"

The man said, "Who, me?"

"Don't you pick on Herbert," said a tall man with a broken nose. "He's daft, anyway."

"That's right," said Herbert. "I'm not responsible for my actions. So watch it."

"You'll have to pump those flats up, won't you?" said the tall man. "Always supposing you brought a pump with you, that is."

Jonas walked in silence around to the back of the car. He unlocked the trunk and found the hand pump. No one tried to stop him. No one said anything. He could feel their hatred. It was not hot, like Sam Barming's. It was controlled and cold.

As he stooped to fix the pump to the first of the tires, there was a slight shuffle of sound behind him. The kick, delivered with a heavy boot, landed just below the base of his spine and pitched him forward against the body of the car.

The pain and the shock waves which followed it nearly blacked him out. He had one thought in his head. The men were going to kill him. In a blind instinct of self-preservation he rolled up against the wheel of the car. He had no idea how long he lay there. It might have been seconds, it might have been whole minutes. All he knew was that no one was touching him.

He put up a hand to wipe away the blood which was running in a steady stream from the gash in his forehead.

Someone was saying something, and he thought that it was a voice he recognized.

He got his free hand onto the ground and pushed himself into a sitting position. No one was looking at him.

A second car, a big dark blue sedan, coming in the other

direction, had drawn up almost level with the hood of his car; and the men were clustering around it, listening to the man who had climbed out. As his eyes started to focus again, he saw that it was Will Dylan.

He heard scraps of talk. "Won't do me any good. Won't do you any good. Get those tires blown up and put the car off the road. I'll take him with me."

"Tell him not to come back, Will," said a voice. "He might not be so lucky next time."

This brought a laugh. The men seemed suddenly remarkably good-tempered.

The blue car pulled forward beside Jonas. A hand came down, caught him by the arm, and pulled him up. The movement caused a pain in his back that made him cry out.

"He's saying thank you," said the voice that had spoken before. Jonas could locate the speaker now. It was the man with the broken nose. "Thank you for a Todmoor welcome."

As Dylan helped him into the front seat of the car, the men stared at him with no more hostility than children show for a Guy Fawker they have hoisted onto a bonfire.

"You'd better use this towel to clean your face up," said Dylan. He had climbed into the driver's seat.

"My car," said Jonas. The words came out like a croak.

"What about it?"

"Not mine. I hired it. Phillips in Sheffield."

"That's all right. There's a garage in Hathersage. We'll stop there and get them to pick it up. I thought so. Here it comes."

There was a smack of heavy raindrops on the roof of the car, and the windshield was suddenly veiled with water. Dylan switched on his wipers and his headlights and drove steadily into the downpour.

The drumming of rain on the roof made all conversation impossible, and for this small mercy Jonas was thankful.

On that Monday morning, at about the time that Jonas' train was drawing into Sheffield Central Station, Mr. Stukely arrived in Wimbledon. A man of leisure, one would have said, with a little business to attend to, but no urgency about it.

He paid visits to both the banks, the London and Home Counties and the Investors and Suburban, which had offices in or near Coalporter Street. He seemed to be expected, for in each of them he had a short talk with the manager. After that he refreshed himself with a cup of coffee and turned his steps to the town hall, where he had some inquiries to make. After which, opening time having arrived, he made his way to the Adam and Eve public house at the end of Coalporter Street and ordered a glass of beer. Here he fell into conversation with a young man who worked at Messrs. Crompton and Maudling, Auctioneers and Estate Agents. Mr. Stukely was an easy talker and seemed to get along equally well with waitresses, barmen, town hall officials and chance-met characters.

At half past two he approached the offices of Jonas Killey. Young Willoughby had come back from his lunch ten minutes before, as Mr. Stukely well knew, having watched him from the saloon bar of the Adam and Eve. He climbed the narrow linoleum-covered steps, rang the bell, and went in.

Mrs. Warburton smiled kindly on him, regretted that Mr. Killey was up north on business, and wondered whether he would like to have a word with Mr. Willoughby. Mr. Stukely said that he would indeed like to do so and was ushered into Jonas' room. It was three minutes before Willoughby appeared, and in that short time Mr. Stukely, who knew a good deal about lawyers' offices, had absorbed a quantity of useful information from the letters and papers which had been left lying about on Jonas' desk. One communication from a firm of builders he found particularly interesting.

When Willoughby arrived, Mr. Stukely explained his business.

He had been recommended to them, he said, by Edward Lambard of Sexton and Lambard, Solicitors, of High Holborn. Mr. Lambard was a personal friend and would himself have handled his business had he not been engaged in the Restrictive Practices Court. He had mentioned Mr. Killey as an expert in trust work, and since he, Mr. Stukely, had other business to transact in Wimbledon, this had fitted in very well. Meanwhile perhaps Mr. Willoughby could take his instructions. Willoughby, impressed by the appearance and manner of his new client, selected a clean sheet of paper and prepared to make notes.

Mr. Stukely desired to set up a trust for his three children. The eldest, a boy, lived in America. Would that complicate matters? Willoughby was not sure, but said he would find out. The other two lived with his wife—not their mother, his second wife—in Buckinghamshire. Willoughby's pen scoured the paper.

At the end of a busy and enjoyable half hour he said, "There's only one thing, Mr. Stukely. You haven't told me how much you wish to settle."

"I had it in mind," said Mr. Stukely, "to make an immediate settlement—there will be more to add to it later, you understand—but an immediate settlement of £20,000. And since you really know nothing about me, I thought it prudent to bring a bank draft for that amount. I obtained it this morning from the local branch of the London and Home Counties Bank. Incidentally, the manager told me that you kept your account there yourselves."

"We keep our client account there."

"Your client account?"

"The Law Society encourages solicitors to keep their office account—that is, their own private money—and their client account—which handles their clients' money—in separate banks. It is not laid down as an absolute rule, but it is very much favored. An additional precaution, you understand, against the two becoming mixed."

Mr. Stukely nodded his head approvingly. He thought it was a very sensible precaution. He said, "I suppose you handle a lot of clients' money."

"Quite a lot," said Willoughby modestly. Most of their clients were tradesmen who wanted debts collected, and young couples who bought houses with building society mortgages. Even so there was a reasonable balance in the client account as a whole, and Willoughby could not help feeling thankful that it was the London and Home Counties Bank which this important new client had visited and not the Investors and Suburban, where the unpleasant Mr. Grimwade kept a jaundiced eye on their overdrawn office balance.

Mr. Stukely said, "I mustn't take up any more of your time. There's no great hurry about the paper work. I am flying over to America tomorrow to visit my son and I shall be away for about ten days. Perhaps we could fix up a second conference when I return. I should like to have a word with Mr. Killey. Not that I haven't every confidence in your expertise, Mr. Willoughby. Wednesday or Thursday week. I can't be more definite until I know about flight times. Suppose I give you a ring when I get back. Excellent."

Mrs. Warburton showed Mr. Stukely out. She actually quit her sanctum to open the door for him, and she was rewarded with a smile.

"Now that's what I call a client," she said to Deborah, the sixteen-year-old girl who did all the jobs in the office that Mrs. Warburton was too busy or too dignified to put her hand to. Deborah agreed that Mr. Stukely was a perfect gentleman. Distinguished too. "Something in the City, I expect," she said. It was encounters of this sort which added luster to the job of working in a solicitor's office and enabled her to upstage her friends who had much better-paid jobs in supermarkets and sweet shops.

That same afternoon Patrick Mauger asked for a few minutes of his editor's time.

John Charles was halfway through the long span of his editorship, which had changed the *Watchman* from a provincial daily to a national newspaper. He was a man of deceptively casual habits. The amount of leisure which he enjoyed derived from his ability to delegate; but everyone, from the latest-joined messenger to the senior news editor, recognized that, in the last analysis, the integrity and repute of the paper depended on decisions that he alone had to make.

He listened carefully to what Patrick had to say. He had a good opinion of his ability, enjoyed his enthusiasm, and mistrusted his judgment.

"Do you think there's anything in it?" he said.

"The story about Will Dylan, you mean? I've no idea. And I don't think it's the real point."

"All right," said Charles patiently. "What is the point?"

"I was in court on Friday. My shorthand's a bit rusty, but I managed to get down almost every word that was said. Particularly that last bit, where Lyon gave him an unnecessary kick in the crutch. And I was watching Killey's face. He's not going to let this matter drop."

"What can he do?"

"There must be some sort of appeal."

"I'll ask our legal eagles about that. Suppose he does appeal, do you think he's any chance of getting whatever it is he wants?"

"I shouldn't think so. But I'm perfectly certain of one thing. He's building up for some sort of showdown. Either he's going to say something quite outrageous about Dylan, who'll be forced to sue him for libel. Or else he'll get the order he wants, and the thing will have to be thrashed out in a criminal court. Even then I don't see him getting a conviction, but think of the publicity."

"What you're saying is that there's a bandwagon going to roll. Do we want to book an early seat on it?"

"I didn't mean to put it quite as crudely as that."

"But that's what you think?"

"More or less."

"Your ears are twitching. You've got some plan in your head. What do you want to do?"

"Almost every other paper has taken the obvious line. Killey's a publicity seeker. Throwing dirt to see if any of it will stick. Got a black eye from the magistrate. Serves him right."

"So?"

"So I'd like to write something a bit different. Not exactly suggesting that there might be something in it. That'd be going too far. But putting both sides of the case."

Charles thought about it. He was far too experienced to believe in the old gag about any publicity being good publicity. Newspapers had been run on such lines, had blossomed for a lush summer, and been blown away by the cold winds of autumn. He had no intention of allowing the *Watchman* to go down that street. What this infatuated young man of his was suggesting was a *ballon d'essai*. A thing which a meteorologist looses into the air to find which way the wind is blowing. A child's toy. He had himself launched many such balloons. Sometimes they had been helpful, often they had drifted away unobserved into the stratosphere. Once or twice they had burst in his face.

He said, "You can write it, but I don't promise we'll publish it. I'll make my mind up about that when I've read it myself."

As Patrick was going, he added, "Have your shorthand notes of the hearing typed out. I want to see those too."

Jonas caught an early train from Sheffield, breakfasted on it, and got to Wimbledon by ten. The left-hand side of his face was bruised and swollen and a strip of pink sticking plaster covered a long cut running from under his left ear to the point of his chin.

Mrs. Warburton said, "Good gracious, Mr. Killey, what *have* you been doing?"

"Slight accident," said Jonas. "Nothing serious. Have you got the Law List?"

"I believe Mr. Willoughby has it."

"Ask him to bring it in, would you? And do you think you could manage me a cup of coffee?"

Mrs. Warburton plugged in the electric kettle and went along to Willoughby's room. She said, "He's back, and he's in a shocking state. Looks as if he's been in a fight. And he wants the Law List."

"Maybe he wants to consult a good solicitor."

"You'd better hurry. I don't think he's in a mood for jokes."

Willoughby refrained from comment when he saw Jonas' face, although it was sufficiently startling. He said, "One or two things have been happening while you've been away. We've got a new client. Rather promising sort of business."

He told him about Mr. Stukely. Jonas listened with half an ear and said, "Good. Good." He had found the number he wanted, and said into the extension, "Get me Holborn 3666, Mrs. Warburton, would you."

SNYDER, RICHARD

Phone: 845-512-8742
Expiration Date: 12/17/2020 11:56 AM

Barcode: 31019011830885
Title: Flash point
Call Number: MYSTERY

RICHARD

SNADER

"Twenty thousand pounds down. A bank draft. I put it on deposit for the time being."

"Quite right."

"We've been having a bit of trouble with Poynters."

"Who?"

"The people who did the conversion here."

"Oh yes. I believe they wrote to me. What do they want now?"

"Money. Just under four hundred pounds. They're getting a bit shirty about it."

"Pay them something on account."

"That's the trouble. I don't think old Grimwade is going to carry us much farther."

"Nonsense," said Jonas. "He's got plenty of security. If he won't accommodate us, we'll move the account to a bank that will. Yes?"

"It's your number, Mr. Killey."

"Thank you. I'd like to speak to Mr. Lambard. The name is Killey."

There was a fairly long pause, and then Edward Lambard's voice, neutral and unsurprised. "What can I do for you?"

"I'd like to come along and consult you. Professionally."

"Does dog eat dog? When would you like to come?"

"I'd be happy to leave it to you to suggest a time. I imagine you're busier than I am."

"I very much doubt it. Should we say tomorrow afternoon at three o'clock."

"That will do very well." Jonas added, with an effort, "It's good of you."

On Wednesday afternoon Patrick produced a first draft of his article and had it torn to pieces by John Charles' own hands. "It leans far too heavily on Killey's side," he said. "Also it's too long, and it's got too many adverbs in it." Adverbs were John Charles' particular *bête noire*. Patrick spent Wednesday evening rewriting it and had it thrown back again. "Now you've made it sound like a pro-Establishment pamphlet." The red-ink note concluded, "Also you have used the word 'basic' three times. On the first occasion you meant 'real,' on the second 'essential,' and on the third nothing in particular."

On Thursday Patrick sat down to write the article again. He was not disheartened. He realized that he was being paid a rare compliment.

Jonas arrived at the offices of Sexton and Lambard in good time. He was not kept waiting. Edward Lambard rose from his chair when he was shown in, advanced the three steps to meet him which he accorded to every client, great or small, said, "Sit where you'll be most comfortable," and sat down himself.

Jonas said, "You heard what happened when I made my application in the Magistrates Court. I've decided to apply to the High Court for an order of mandamus. It seems to be the only way of forcing him to treat my application properly. I can't handle it myself. That's why I've come to you."

Mongoose was right, thought Lambard. If you miss with your first bite, go after the snake again.

He said, "You'll need counsel. Leading counsel, for an application of that sort, I should think."

Jonas nodded.

"And that will cost money."

"How much?"

It was a question solicitors are always being asked and can never answer.

"Leave my fees out of it for the moment," said Lambard. "It'll be a short hearing. Say a single morning. Leading counsel, a junior, a certain number of papers. A verbatim report of the hearing at West London would be useful. Did you have a short-hand writer in court?"

"I'm afraid not."

"I'm only guessing. But you might be able to do it for five hundred pounds."

"I see," said Jonas bleakly. "If I can raise five hundred pounds, you'll handle it for me?"

"I didn't say so. All I was doing was telling you what I thought it would cost you. I very much doubt if I can undertake it."

"Why not?"

"A fair question. Before I answer it, I'll put one to you. You seem willing to lay out five hundred pounds of your own money. There'll be no question of recovering costs even if you succeed. You won't get a penny of it back. What are you doing it for?"

It was the second time in three days that he had been asked the question. Since he disliked Edward Lambard, he had that much less hesitation in answering it. He said, "I think that certain members of the Anglo-Scottish Independent Aluminium Company were defrauded of a portion of their hard-earned savings. They are in no position to take action for themselves. I happen to be in a position to help them. I propose to do so."

"How much would you say was involved?"

"Involved?"

"Let me put it more crudely. How much do you think Dylan stole?"

"It's difficult to say. Somewhere between four hundred and eight hundred pounds."

"Let's take the higher figure." Lambard jotted it down. "I believe there are about four thousand men working in the smelter now. So each of them lost—let me see—twenty new pence."

"You can't look at it mathematically."

"I always look at mathematical problems mathematically," said Lambard. "Now what you're telling me is that you feel so strongly about a workman who lost twenty pence that you're prepared to spend five hundred pounds trying to get it back for him. Even though those same workmen kicked you in the face on Monday."

Jonas said, "How—"

"Perhaps you haven't had time to read the papers today. The incident was reported in the Sheffield *Courier* on Wednesday, and the London papers picked it up this morning. Just at this moment you're news."

He pushed across a copy of the *Daily Telegraph* folded open at the inside of the front page and Jonas saw the headline "Solicitor Mobbed."

He skimmed through the account. It implied, using the carefully guarded double-talk of the press, that he had visited the smelter at Todmoor "in search of further evidence," and had provoked the workmen by making tactless remarks about Will Dylan, "who is, of course, a highly respected figure in those parts."

"It's totally inaccurate," he said. "It wasn't anything like that at all."

"But it was the ASIA workers who gave you that bruise on your face?"

"Yes."

"And you still want them to get their twenty pence back?"

"Now you're being stupid," said Jonas. When he argued, a pressure built up inside him which made him say things which his own cooler reason rejected even while he was saying them. "Either you really don't understand what all this is about, or you're pretending not to understand it so that you can have an excuse to wash your hands of it. Of course it's not the money. It's the principle."

"What principle exactly?" said Lambard.

He had his pen in his hand and looked blandly over his glasses at Jonas as though he was preparing to write down his answer word for word.

Jonas swallowed and said, "It's the principle that the law is the law, and no matter how powerful the lawbreaker is, or how long ago he broke it, or however small the actual sum involved, he must be brought to trial."

"All right," said Lambard. "That's a principle which any lawyer ought to be able to accept. I think it's a counsel of perfection, but let that go. The mistake you're making is a common mistake with amateur logicians. You're building on a faulty premise. Everything you have said holds good *if* the law has been broken. It does not necessarily hold good merely because you *suspect* that the law has been broken. As far as I can gather, that's what the magistrate was telling you. Maybe he wasn't very tactful about it. But that was the message he was trying to get over. Prove that a crime has been committed. Prove it beyond reasonable doubt, and the law must help you to extract the appropriate penalty. But don't start slinging mud in the hope that the law will help you to make some of it stick."

Jonas had twice made angry noises at the back of his throat, but a lingering habit of deference to the man who had once been his employer had restrained him. Now he got to his feet, the bruise on his cheek livid against a white face, and said in a strangled tone of voice, "I take it then, that you won't help me."

"I'm afraid that's right," said Lambard.

The managing director of Messrs. Poynters ("Builders and Decorators. Conversions Our Specialty") looked at the card and at the insignificant man who had proferred it, and he said, "It seems mad to me, but I can't see the catch, Mr. Raven."

"No catch at all," said Terence. "You get your money; we get our money. That's what the Raven Service is all about."

"You'll pay me the whole of what Mr. Killey owes me."

"Less the discount you would have given him for a cash settlement. Five per cent, I understand."

"Then what do you get out of it?"

"We collect the lot. So the discount goes to us."

The managing director made a quick calculation. Five per

cent of four hundred was twenty pounds. The little man was offering to collect his debt for him for twenty pounds. It seemed a reasonable bargain.

"It's a deal," he said. "What do you want me to do?"

"Just sign this paper transferring the debt to us. I give you a certified check." He produced paper and check from his brief case and laid them on the desk.

As the managing director was about to sign, a thought struck him.

"How are you going to collect?" he said. "Mr. Killey's been pretty difficult about paying us. He's going to be even more difficult when he finds someone else has bought up the debt."

"The Raven Service," said Terence, "has its own methods."

Patrick's article appeared on Friday morning. It was printed on the left-hand center page, opposite the leader, and was subtitled "A Case for Thought."

At first reading it appeared to be a general criticism of the arbitrary power of a magistrate to refuse an application for a summons on what, as the article put, "must appear to a layman to be mere legalistic grounds." Because a copy of a document was produced rather than an original, or a print of a photograph and not the negative, must a citizen be refused his primary right to pursue justice? Such niceties should surely be reserved for the hearing of the case itself.

As an illustration of this, indeed almost as an afterthought, the facts of Jonas Killey's application were mentioned.

The editors of Fleet Street, who daily observe the developments of their rivals with the absorbed intensity of a mother watching for the first signs of pregnancy in a suspect daughter, said in unison to their assistant editors, "The *Watchman's* up to something. Keep an eye on it." Lobby correspondents were consulted and said, in similar unison, "We don't think there's anything in it. But better wait and see."

Christopher Martingale read the article in the train on his

way up to London and thought that Patrick had written it rather well. It was mercifully free from some of his usual verbal flourishes. Here, had he known it, he was paying tribute to the blue pencil of John Charles.

The Minister for Labor, Bernard Gracey, read the article and disliked it. He said as much to Air Vice-Marshal Pulleyne, whom he had summoned to his house in St. John's Wood.

"It's a try-on," he said.

"Sailing a bit close to the wind," said Pulleyne.

"Can they comment like this on a decision of the court? Give names and details?"

"I've no idea, Minister."

"Ask Benz-Fisher. He's a lawyer. You'll be seeing him about it, I imagine."

"I think I shall have to," said Pulleyne.

He sounded so unenthusiastic that Gracey looked up and said, "You don't approve of him, do you?"

"I don't disapprove of him," said Pulleyne. "It's just that he's out of this world. The ordinary rules don't apply to him any longer. He makes up his own rules. There were one or two people like him in the Air Force. They killed themselves sooner or later, but they sometimes killed a lot of other people first." There was something else that had to be said, and after a suitable pause Pulleyne said it. "I take it, Minister, that you want this business quashed."

"I do."

"And that is an order?"

"It is."

Gracey said it angrily. Pulleyne, who was a student of how men behaved under pressure, thought that the anger had a touch of apprehension behind it.

He telephoned Benz-Fisher that morning and invited him round to the Ministry of Defense. Benz-Fisher said, "I don't think it would be a terribly good idea if I were to be seen going into a place like that. It might give people ideas. If you don't want to come round to my office, let's meet on neutral ground. There's a nice little pub on the corner of Petty France and Picton Street. It's called the Battle of Salamanca. No one much in the private bar before lunch. Meet you there in twenty minutes."

He rang off before Pulleyne could frame an objection.

The décor of the private bar of the Battle of Salamanca was much to Benz-Fisher's taste. The Iron Duke, at that period a mere Earl, stared down his nose at Marshal Marmont. The marshal bore a striking resemblance to Alf Ramsey and looked subdued. Possibly he realized that his team was going to be beaten. Other pictures had been related with equal care to the battle. Over the fireplace Wellington addressed Sir Edward Pakenham. "Move on with the Third Division and drive everything before you." On the wall opposite the window General Le Marchant, at the head of a thousand sabers, fell like a bolt from the blue upon the disorganized infantry of General Mancune.

Benz-Fisher placed himself at the head of the charge and drew his own saber. Then, remembering that Le Marchant had fallen in the moment of victory, he substituted himself for Pakenham, who had had an equally satisfactory battle but had managed to survive it.

"I know of no room in which beer tastes better," said Benz-Fisher. "In this country patriotism and the brewing industry have always gone hand in hand. But perhaps you are not a student of the Peninsular War?"

"Great stuff," said Pulleyne. "The pictures, I mean. I won't drink beer, if you don't mind. A gin and tonic would do splendidly. A bit of ice, if they can manage it, but no lemon."

He was casting an eye around the small room as he spoke. His main reason for refusing to visit Benz-Fisher in his office was that he was aware that his conversation would be recorded. He was wondering whether this room also had been wired for sound. Benz-Fisher read his thoughts accurately. He said, "If you would feel more comfortable in the public bar—"

"No, no. This will do excellently."

"No microphones, I assure you."

"Such a thought never crossed my mind. But you do appreciate that what I have to say is completely confidential."

"You mean," said Benz-Fisher, "that if whatever it is you want me to do goes wrong, you'll deny ever having told me to do it."

"Exactly."

"Would I be wide of the mark if I surmised that a certain fluttering in official dovecotes has been caused by an article in this morning's *Watchman.*"

"You'd be dead right."

"And that this is all part of the problem which you expounded to me in my office last week."

"It's a development of that problem. Have you been able to do anything about it?"

"Employing the sort of phraseology which this room suggests, I would say that I have planned a broad strategy, made certain tactical preparations, and moved elements of my forces into position."

"I'm not asking for any details," said Pulleyne hastily. "The fact is, the old man's getting worried. I'd guess he's planning to hold the election in the early autumn. He'll announce it soon after the House rises at the end of next month."

There was a pause while the drinks arrived. Benz-Fisher lowered half of the contents of the silver tankard which the landlord kept aside for his personal use and said, "One does appreciate that at this particular moment even a minor scandal could be an embarrassment. Particularly if it is of the sort of scandal that the opposition press could take up."

"If it was anyone but Dylan," said Pulleyne gloomily, "it wouldn't be so bad. But he's a sort of mascot. A key figure. Any attack on him which got off the ground could be terribly damaging."

"And you want me to see that it doesn't get off the ground?"

108

"We want it deflated. We want the whole thing cut down to size."

"And you want me to do the cutting?"

"You're not to do anything"—the Air Vice-Marshal paused, selecting his next word as carefully as if he was choosing the card to lead in a high-stakes game of bridge—"anything outrageous."

Benz-Fisher bared his teeth in a terrifying grin. "Ask not the butcher which knife he will appoint. Let *him* cut up the carcass. *You* enjoy the joint."

"Oh quite," said Pulleyne.

"All I need is the order to begin."

"You have it."

"Mon cher Alava," said Benz-Fisher, *"Marmont est perdu."*

Patrick much enjoyed a walk across London in the small hours of the morning when the streets were quiet and almost deserted. London, he had noticed, never quite went to sleep. Early risers crossed with belated revelers. Home-going cars drew aside to let through the great lorries which rolled into market at Covent Garden. An occasional policeman patrolled the empty pavements or stood in a doorway watching the night go by.

It had been an exciting evening. First, and most important, they had won the Beaverbrook trophy, defeating the *Daily Express* in the third of three hotly contested legs. Even the redoubtable Pearly Deans had failed to stop them. When the pub had finally put up its shutters and turned victors and vanquished alike into the street, a move had been made to a drinking club in Farringdon Road of which Lefty Marks seemed to be a member. The club was short of beer but had reasonable stocks of whisky and a broad-minded interpretation of licensing hours.

It was two o'clock when Patrick finally emerged and set out on his long stroll across the town, setting his course northward and westward toward Regent's Park. It took him fifteen minutes to reach the end of High Holborn, and here he turned to the right and plunged into the haphazard arrangement of small streets which surround the British Museum. He had no fear of losing his way. If he kept taking the first turning to the left and the first to the right, he must eventually strike the Euston Road.

The girl was sitting on the sand bin at the end of Rickaby Street. She had her shoes off and was looking at her stockinged feet; one stocking had a large hole in the toe.

As Patrick came up, she wriggled her toe at him and said, "See that. Fifty pence the pair and worn out almost as soon as I put them on."

"Bad luck," said Patrick. He thought the girl couldn't have been more than sixteen. He sat down on the other end of the sand bin.

"They don't make stockings like they used to," said the girl. "In my grandmother's day they knitted them out of wool and wire."

"Wire? Are you sure?"

"Wire," said the girl firmly. "Every fifth strand was wire. She had a pair which lasted for forty years. She had to give them up in the end."

"Why?"

"They were an unfashionable color. You haven't got a cigarette by any chance? I've got through all mine."

Patrick got out his case. The girl said, "Thanks," took one, and got out her own lighter.

"Aren't you a bit young to be a regular smoker?" said Patrick. "Have you got any idea what it does to your lungs?"

"No. Tell."

"It coats the delicate membranes with nicotine tar."

"Is that a bad thing? I thought tar was healthy. In the old days, when they cut your leg off, they smeared tar all over the stump. Did you know?"

"Who told you that? Your grandmother?"

The girl started to laugh, and stopped suddenly. Then Patrick saw the two men. They had come up behind him, walking very quietly. They were not large, but stocky. They were bare-headed. One of them had a round bald patch at the back of his head which Patrick noticed when he turned to address the girl. He said, "You'd better be getting along home."

The girl said, "I'm quite happy here." But she swung her legs down and pushed her feet into her shoes. Her voice was not as confident as her words.

"Stop bullying the girl," said Patrick. "She's doing no harm."

The men ignored him. The second one, who was younger and had a razor-cut mustache, said, "You oughtn't to be out as late as this. Just get along home."

The girl looked uncertain. The men looked at her and said nothing. As she started to move away, she gave Patrick an apologetic look as if to say, "I'm sorry, but you see how it is."

Patrick had been getting steadily angrier, but the look pulled him up short. It suddenly occurred to him that the men were waiting for the girl to go before they started on their real business. And he had an uncomfortable idea of what that business might be. The street was completely deserted, and his wallet, which had quite a few pounds in it, was burning a hole in his pocket.

As if to confirm his suspicions, bald patch took a step forward.

Patrick dived to one side, avoided a grabbing hand, and started to run. The young man was quicker than he was. He collared Patrick from behind and they went down together, with Patrick underneath. As he hit the pavement, he rolled and brought his head forward. The top of his forehead smashed into his opponent's face and he heard a gasp of pain. Then hands grabbed him by the hair and jerked him up into a kneeling position. A foot landed in his stomach, driving all the wind out of him.

He was aware that a car had driven up and stopped almost on top of him. The next moment he was in the back seat, wedged between his two opponents. The driver looked back at them as he engaged gear. Patrick saw that he was a uniformed policeman. He was grinning. "That's a lovely shiner you've got, Sammy," he said.

"It's nothing to what he's going to get," said the young man. Bald patch said, "Get cracking. We don't want to be all night about it, do we?"

"My name," said bald patch, "is Donald McGillivray. I am a detective sergeant attached to 'J' Division of the Metropolitan Police for special duties. In connection with those duties I was making a routine patrol with Detective Roper in the area of Anderby Street at approximately two A.M. yesterday morning."

"Yesterday, Sergeant?"

"I am sorry, sir. I mean, of course, this morning. I observed the accused annoying a young girl. She was obviously annoyed and frightened by what he was doing—"

"That's a lie," said Patrick.

Mr. Gazelee, the magistrate, turned his head to look at him. Patrick was aware that he was not looking his best. He was unshaven and a wash in cold water with a scrap of yellow soap had spread rather than removed the dirt of the night. His collar had burst and was loosely held together by what was left of his tie. He had been sick twice during the hours he had spent in his cell and on the second occasion had not entirely avoided soiling his clothes.

Mr. Gazelee said, "You will have an opportunity of giving the court your own version at the proper time. If you interrupt again, I will have you removed, and the case will proceed in your absence. Yes, officer?"

"Well, sir. We thought we ought to intervene. When we did so, the accused became violent and struck Detective Roper—"

"He will tell us about that."

"Yes, sir. Then we apprehended him and took him to Gray's Inn Road police station."

"Had he been drinking?"

"In my opinion, sir, yes. He smelled strongly of drink and I understand that he vomited during the night. He was offered an opportunity of taking a breathalizer test but refused."

The magistrate looked at Mr. Billinghay, who said, "I have no questions." Mr. Billinghay was the *Watchman*'s own legal adviser. He knew everything about copyright and defamation and nothing about the criminal law. An urgent telephone call had dragged him away from his breakfast. He looked as unhappy as Patrick.

Detective Roper entered the box and repeated the evidence of his colleague in words so similar that they had the effect of a carbon copy. He had a beautiful black eye.

Mr. Billinghay said, "Are you saying that he hit you with his fist?"

"It's difficult in a scrap to say what you're being hit with," said Detective Roper. He had an open and boyish smile. "I certainly thought it was his fist."

"But he could have done it accidentally with his head."

"I can only say it didn't seem accidental to me."

"Well, Mr. Billinghay?"

"I should like my client to give the court his own story."

"Very well. He can make a statement from the dock. Or he can make it under oath from the witness box. In which case he will be subject to cross-examination."

"From the witness box," said Patrick firmly.

He was aware that he presented a ludicrous sight, that the court would be totally disinclined to believe him, and that the course of wisdom would have been to say as little as possible. But his anger had cleared his head and he had got his voice back.

He said, "I was walking home from a darts match. I had had a certain amount to drink, but I was not drunk. This girl stopped me by asking me for a cigarette. We had a few minutes' talk. There was no question of me propositioning her or annoying her in any way. Then these two men came up. They told the girl to clear off. I think she was frightened of them. I certainly was. There was nothing to show they were policemen. They didn't say they were, or produce warrant cards or anything like that. As soon as they had got rid of the girl they closed in on me."

"Are you telling the court," said Mr. Gazelee, "that they assaulted you?"

"They didn't have a chance. I took to my heels. One of them caught me from behind and collared me. In the mix-up I think my head hit his. I've certainly got a very sore place on my forehead."

"Can you suggest any reason why these two officers should have assaulted you?"

There were a number of possible answers to this, and almost all of them would have been dangerous. Patrick had his wits about him by now. He said, "I have no idea, sir."

Mr. Gazelee thought about it, running a finger down the side of his face. Then he said, "Yes, Inspector?"

The uniformed police inspector who was conducting the prosecution said, "I have no questions, sir."

"Has any effort been made to trace this girl?"

"An effort has been made, sir. But in the time available it was not successful."

Mr. Gazelee thought about it again. He had very little doubt about what had happened. The unpleasant young oaf had got tight, had annoyed a girl and assaulted a policeman. Since it was a first offense, the short sharp sentence of imprisonment which he would like to have given him would not do. It would have to be a fine. Quite a heavy fine. However, it would do him good to have a few days to wonder about it.

He said, "I think that a further effort should be made to obtain her testimony. I shall remand the case for this day week."

"I take it there will be no objection to bail. I have the authority of my employers to offer any necessary sum—"

"There's no need to make an issue of it, Mr. Billinghay. He will be released on his own recognizance."

"I will *not* conduct a crusade on your behalf," said John Charles.

"No, sir," said Patrick.

"You will turn up next week in your best blue suit and your regimental tie and say that you have decided, on reflection, to change your plea to guilty."

"Guilty?" said Patrick, outraged.

"Certainly."

"But the whole thing was a put-up job."

"What difference does that make?"

"What difference—"

"If you were framed, you were neatly and effectively framed. You are going to be found guilty, whatever you say or do. The only way you can make it any worse is by making a fuss about it and attracting a great deal of publicity, most of it unfavorable."

"If we could find that girl—"

"How do you suggest we set about it? Advertise for her? Or make it a front-page story, 'The Missing Witness.' My dear Patrick, you'd be playing straight into their hands."

"Then you do think there was something fishy about it?"

"I didn't say so. But if it was and the girl was in it, she'll be very unlikely to turn up, don't you think?"

"She can't have been in it," said Patrick slowly. "It's quite impossible. I was drifting home at random. First right, first left. No one could possibly have predicted which way I was going to take."

"Then how do you suggest they did it?"

"One thing I noticed at the time was how quietly they moved. Thick crepe rubber soles, I imagine. I think they'd been following me ever since I left that club. Even earlier, maybe. They'd only got to keep one turning behind me. When I stopped to talk to that girl, it gave them just the chance they wanted."

"And if you hadn't stopped?"

"All they had to do was catch up and make a pass at me. I'd naturally assume they were a couple of muggers. I could only run or fight back. Either way I was for it. It was too damned easy."

"I see," said John Charles. "And the object of the exercise?"

Patrick shifted uncomfortably. He said, "It did occur to me that my article may have upset . . . someone."

"Yes?"

"If I do a follow-up on it, people are going to say, 'That's just that stupid young bugger who picked up the tart and sloshed a policeman.' "

"And who do you suggest is the 'someone' you've annoyed?"

"I don't exactly know. The government perhaps."

John Charles smiled for the first time that morning. He said, "I think you overrate the effectiveness of your literary efforts, Patrick. And anyway, suppose we're right. Aren't you making things a hundred times worse if you fight? I understand there was only one man in court. He was from the *Evening Banner*. We can see that he forgets about it."

Patrick nodded. The *Banner* was a subsidiary of the *Watchman*.

"Plead guilty next week, and that kills the story dead."

"All right," said Patrick unhappily.

Mutt told Christopher all about it that evening.

"It was a plot," she said. "A nasty sneaky put-up job. It's all very well for Charlie-boy to order Patrick to plead guilty. Suppose Dreyfus had pleaded guilty."

"I don't think the two cases are really comparable."

"All injustices are comparable," Mutt said inexorably.

They were lying in bed. It was where they had their serious conversations.

"It doesn't seem to have occurred to anyone that those two coppers may simply have been filling up their books."

"Meaning what?"

"It's said to be helpful to your prospects of promotion if you have a fair number of arrests to your credit."

"I don't believe it," said Mutt.

An owl echoed her incredulity from the garden.

"Anyway," he said sleepily, "if you're right and it was a put-up job in order to smear Patrick publicly and take the sting out of anything he meant to write, it didn't come off."

"What do you mean?"

"No publicity."

But that was before they saw the *Independent* on Wednesday morning.

"The Missing Witness," said the front-page headline, exactly as John Charles had predicted. And underneath, "Find This Girl."

Patrick read it on his way to work and was not surprised when he was intercepted in the foyer by Charles' secretary. She said, "Go straight up, for God's sake. Don't bother about your things. I'll look after them. The old man's behaving like a caged lion."

Charles was not actually pacing the floor. He rarely gave visible evidence of his feelings, but it was clear that he was very angry. He said, "Sit down. We've got to think about this. I've had a word with our chap on the *Banner,* and he's certain there were none of the regulars in court. These chaps all know each other. That means they had an unknown reporter there, probably in the public section. And that means that it *was* a put-up job. If they think I'm going to sit down under it, they can think again."

Patrick was not clear whether Charles was angry that a story which was his by rights had been snatched from under his nose, or that one of his own staff had been put on the spot, or that his judgment had been proved at fault. He made a neutral but encouraging noise.

"Of course, it would be the *Independent.* We all know

what *their* politics are. Party lap dogs."

"Suppose they actually find the girl," said Patrick. "Won't that upset the apple cart?"

"They've made damned certain she won't turn up. You said she was a well-spoken sort of girl."

"Middle class. Possibly upper middle."

"And now the *Independent* is suggesting that either you propositioned her or she propositioned you. In other words that she was a tart. Or you mistook her for one. Do you think she's going to step forward voluntarily into that sort of much?"

"They might trace her."

"How? No one's got a description that wouldn't fit two million other girls."

"Inquiries in the neighborhood."

"She didn't live in the neighborhood."

"How do you know?"

"If she'd been anywhere near home, she wouldn't have sat down and taken her shoes off to rest her feet."

"I suppose not."

"Forget the girl. We shall have to slug this out in court. If they want a splash, by God we'll give them a splash. We'll get you Marcus Hoyle."

For the first time that morning Patrick really did look shaken. He said, "Are you sure—"

"Just the man for the job. He's upset more judges than anyone else at the bar. 'The mouth of a bell and the heart of Hell and the head of a gallows-tree.' "

Old Mrs. Killey got up long before Jonas, and she had been clattering around in the kitchen for half an hour by the time he put in an appearance. He was halfway through breakfast when the telephone rang.

It was Ben Thomas. He said, "Thought I'd give you the good news. You'll find something for you in the post today. At the office."

"What are you talking about?"

"We got some private inquiry agents moving up north. They've turned up quite a lot of stuff. Good stuff."

"I never told you . . . I mean, I can't possibly afford to pay inquiry agents."

"Yes. That was another thing I had to pass on to you. Don't worry about the money. We've got funds."

"I'm not sure—"

"You'll need money for that appeal of yours. Get the best barrister going. A Q.C. if you like. We can afford it."

"Look here! What *is* all this about? I didn't ask you to interfere in my affairs."

Ben said, in a voice which was suddenly quite free from banter, "We're not interfering, Mr. Killey. We're helping."

"Oh."

"And another thing. I do apologize for ringing you at home, but I think your office line's been bugged."

He rang off, and Jonas sat staring at the receiver. His mother said, "Come on, your coffee's getting cold. Who was that?"

"Business."

"They ought to know better than to ring you up at home. Your father would never allow it. Even when that case of his was on. Not that he ever stopped thinking about it. He used to sit up in bed at night and start addressing the court."

"I wonder how you can tell," said Jonas.

"I was in bed with him."

When he got to the office, he stared for a long time at the telephone on his desk, then he lifted the receiver cautiously and dialed his home number. When his mother answered, he said, "Oh, there's a letter I wrote last night. I left it on the mantelpiece. I meant to post it and forgot."

"I'll do it."

Jonas listened intently. Was there, or was he imagining it, a slight resonance, as though his mother was speaking in a large empty room?

"And Jonas—"

"Yes."

"I didn't mean to worry you, but as you rang up, I thought I'd tell you. I was talking to Mrs. Frampton, who lives next door. She said she'd noticed a man watching the house."

"Her house or ours?"

"She wasn't certain. She said he'd been there two days running. If he turned up again, she was going to tell the police."

"Tell her to do that," said Jonas.

He rang off and tried to concentrate on the work in front of him. He had been away so much that a lot had piled up. Almost the first envelope he opened contained the report of Messrs. Godsall and Ramage ("Credit Inquiries Made. Personal Investigations Undertaken. Writs Served"). It was couched in customarily discreet terms. Following upon instructions from the Client, they had made certain investigations in connection with the Subject, with particular attention to possible proceedings in court during the Period Specified. These had produced positive results in three cases, as per the copy records enclosed.

Jonas examined the records. It was clear from them that Will Dylan had settled three court cases for sums owed by him, one to a garage, one to a builder, and one to a tailor, and all in the period immediately before he left ACAT and joined MG. The only heavy one was the builder. The total sums involved, with costs, came to just under £500.

It was not conclusive, but it was a small and definite fact. Jonas filed the report away and turned with a sigh to the work in front of him. He looked at his diary and saw that someone called Stukely was due to come and see him at three o'clock that afternoon. Stukely? The name meant something. He rang for Mrs. Warburton. She said, "He's that man who came when you were in Sheffield. Such a nice man. Something to do with a trust. Mr. Willoughby spoke to him."

"I remember," said Jonas. "I'll have a word with him. Now, we'd better make a start on this mortgage."

By one o'clock some of the papers had been transferred from his desk to Mrs. Warburton's typing table. He decided to work straight on through the lunch hour. It was true that his private affairs were cutting savagely into the routine of his practice.

At a quarter to two the telephone rang. It was the neighborly Mrs. Frampton, and she sounded upset. She said, "I'm sorry to ring you up like this, but if I don't, I'm sure I don't know who will, and there's been some trouble at your house."

"What sort of trouble?"

"There were two men who came and made a terrible fuss. They were shouting at your mother and carrying on. It can't have done her any good, you know. Not at her age, and with her heart."

Jonas could feel his own heart pumping. He could make very little sense of it all. He said, "What's happening? What's being done?"

"Ah! There's the doctor's car now. He'll look after her."

"For God's sake," said Jonas, "what is it? What's happening? No, don't bother to explain. Tell them I'm coming right back."

He was lucky enough to pick up a taxi in Wimbledon High Street and was at his house twenty minutes later. As he was on the point of paying off the driver, Mrs. Frampton, who had been watching from her own front window, darted out to meet him. She was a large untidy gray-haired kindly woman, flustered to incoherence by the excitement and importance of the occasion. Fortunately her daughter followed her out, and it was from her that Jonas got the story.

At about one o'clock a car had stopped outside the gate, two men had jumped out, and had hammered on Mrs. Killey's front door and rung her bell. When Mrs. Killey appeared, the men had started shouting at her. Bellowing, amended Mrs. Frampton. Then they had pushed roughly past her and gone into the house. There had been sounds of banging and crashing and more shouting, lasting for about five minutes.

"Why the hell didn't someone send for the police?" said Jonas.

"We didn't like to interfere," said Miss Frampton. "It didn't seem to be our business exactly. When they'd gone, Mum went over to see what it was all about. The front door was locked, so she went round the back and found your mother—"

"Poor soul," said Mrs. Frampton. "White as a sheet. Lying back in her chair—"

"And she sent for the doctor. I'm sure I hope she did right."

"Quite right," said Jonas. "I'm sure I'm very grateful. Where is she?"

"The doctor took her down to the Archway Hospital. In his own car."

"White as a sheet," said Mrs. Frampton.

"Hop in. I know where it is," said the taxi driver, who had been listening, fascinated. "I'll run you down."

The doctor was coming out as Jonas arrived. He said, "Are you Mr. Killey? I've given your mother a sedative. She won't be able to talk to you until this evening. She's in a state of shock."

"Did you find out what happened?"

"She told me something about it on the way down. As far as I could make out those two brutes forced their way in and accused her of having stolen a child. They insisted she was hiding it in the house. They stormed up and down, more or less ransacked the place. Of course they didn't find anyone. So they pushed off. Not a pleasant experience for an old lady with a dicky heart."

"Is there anything I can do for her?"

"What I think you ought to do is find her somewhere nice and quiet for the next few weeks. She won't want to go back to that house. Not until she gets her nerve back. Every time the doorbell rings she'll start imagining things."

"I suppose you couldn't keep her here?"

"It'd be next to impossible," said the doctor. "We're so pressed you have to have some medically treatable complaint to hold on to your bed."

"Isn't there a convalescent home?"

"Several. All fairly booked up too. Why don't you have a word with the almoner? If anything can be done, she'll do it for you."

The word "almoner" suggested to Jonas a formidable lady, more dragonlike even than the matrons and sisters who ruled the wards. It was an agreeable surprise to meet a girl of about twenty-five. It was even more surprising when she greeted him by name and said, "I believe you used to work for Daddy, didn't you? It was a few years ago, but I remember seeing you when I came to the office."

He glanced down at the desk and took in the name on the card for the first time. Penelope Lambard. "So you're Edward Lambard's daughter," he said. "I can't pretend I remember you."

"Since I should have been wearing school uniform and had my hair in pigtails, you can be forgiven. Now let's see what we can do for you. Make yourself comfortable. I'll probably have to do a lot of telephoning."

It was nearly two hours later when Jonas left the hospital, but it had been worth the wait. At the sixth effort the helpful Miss Lambard had fixed his mother up with a fortnight's berth at the Woking Nursing Home. She was to stay in hospital for three more days and to move there at the weekend. There would be fees to pay. Jonas had made arrangements about that. He suddenly realized that he was very hungry.

"Go out and get yourself something to eat," said Penelope. "Come back at half past five. The ward sister will have finished her rounds by then, and you ought to be able to see your mother for a few minutes."

He had not known what to expect, and had been surprised and relieved that his mother looked so unchanged. She seemed more worried about him than about herself.

"Don't you fret," he said. "I'm used to looking after myself. I'll get most of my meals out."

As he was leaving, she said, "How are things going with . . . you know?"

"They're going all right."

"Don't you think you might—" His mother stopped. Jonas was uncertain whether it was embarrassment or a twinge of pain. He waited for her to go on, standing at the foot of the bed, and then saw that she had her eyes closed. Alarmed, he went back to her side, but she seemed to be breathing deeply and gently. After a moment or two he stole away.

He walked home, up the long hill under the Archway viaduct, with the sun beginning to throw long shadows across the road. As he opened his front door, he heard the telephone ringing. It was Willoughby. He was too young to disguise the panic in his voice. He said, "I think you ought to come back to the office at once. It's rather serious."

Willoughby had got back from his lunch at a quarter past two. He heard from Mrs. Warburton that Jonas had been called away by a message about his mother, and he said something unkind. It meant that he would have to cope with Mr. Stukely, who would be justifiably disappointed at not seeing Mr. Killey, and might be difficult to handle. Also he had not carried out all the research he ought to have done on the subject of discretionary trusts, relying on the expertise of his senior to carry him through. He hurried to his own room to remedy the deficiency.

His room was next to the top of the stairs, and he could hear visitors as they came up.

"As a result of the 1971 Finance Act it is no longer possible both to distribute income to a beneficiary and to escape estate duty on that beneficiary's death. The legislature . . ."

Footsteps coming up, but not Mr. Stukely. Two men at least, and walking heavily.

He heard the front door being opened ungently and the

sound of voices. Men's voices. Men who were not exactly shouting but were talking very loudly indeed. Mrs. Warburton came in. She was angry, and upset. She said, "You'll have to come and deal with these men, Mr. Willoughby. I can't make out what they want."

The two men were standing in the middle of the small reception room, almost filling it with their aggressive bulk. They wore corduroy trousers and jackets belted at the waist. Willoughby thought they looked like removal men.

As soon as he came into the room, the older man turned on Willoughby and said, "You the guvnor?"

"I'm one of the partners."

"Where's the guvnor then?"

"He's out. What do you—"

The man took two quick steps forward, until he was almost touching Willoughby, and said, "I'll show you what I want." He had a piece of paper in his hand. Willoughby could see the heading, "Raven Services," and something about Messrs. Poynters and a sum of £400 now payable. Before he could read any more, the man had whisked it away. "That's what I want. Four hundred bloody smackers. And we're not going till we get 'em."

"You've got no right to come bursting in here like this. If you want your money, go to court and get an order."

The words were brave, but his voice let him down. Willoughby was worried. He had one eye on the clock. It was twenty to three. Mr. Stukely was due at three o'clock.

"I don't need no more order than this. You owe the money. Right? We've got orders to collect it. If you can't pay in cash we'll take it in kind. That looks like a good typewriter. Say sixty pounds."

Mrs. Warburton gave a squeak of outrage.

"Must be other typewriters here," said the younger man. "Tape recorders too, I expect. We might clear the lot, with a bit of luck." He made a move toward the inner door. Mrs. Warburton flung her arms around her new electric typewriter. Wil-

126

loughby said, "Stop that. They'll have to have the money. Give me the check book."

"We're not all that keen on checks, actually," said the older man. "Like rubber balls. They got a way of bouncing."

"Deborah can go round to the bank with it."

Mrs. Warburton had got two check books out of the drawer in the safe and put them both on her table. After a moment of hesitation, Willoughby took the larger of them and wrote out a check for £400 payable to cash. Deborah, who had been attracted into the room by the noise and seemed to be enjoying the drama, took the check and departed reluctantly.

"Hurry," said Willoughby.

"No hard feelings," said the older man. "Just a job we have to do. Not necessarily agreeable. Like some of your jobs, I expect."

Willoughby had nothing to say to that. They sat in silence until they heard Deborah's footsteps ascending. Other and heavier steps came with her. She was not alone.

Mr. Stukely held the door open for her and followed her in. He said, "I happened to meet this young lady at the bank, and as we were both making for the same destination, I offered to escort her home. She was telling me that you had a little trouble."

"That's quite all right," said Willoughby stiffly. He handed the money to the older man, who counted it carefully, and said, "Dead right. The young lady done a good job. I'll give you a receipt."

He signed the paper he had brought, handed it to Willoughby, winked at Deborah, and led the way out of the room. The younger man shut the door softly behind him. It seemed like a curtain coming down at the end of a violent scene.

Willoughby took a deep breath and said, "I'm sorry that Mr. Killey isn't here. He was called away unexpectedly. However, I think I can bring you up to date with our thoughts on the matter."

Mr. Stukely made no attempt to move. He said, "I too am sorry that Mr. Killey is not here. I imagine that if he were here he would be able to explain something which has been puzzling me ever since I met this young lady at the bank."

Willoughby said, "Oh?" He tried to make it sound like a polite inquiry.

"When I was here last, you gave me an interesting explanation of the rules of the Law Society which govern solicitors' accounts. You told me, correct me if I am wrong, that you kept your own money at the Investors and Suburban Bank and your clients' money quite separately at the London and Home Counties Bank. Right? Now I gathered from my conversation with this young lady that the account you had been called upon to meet was a private account of your own. Builders, wasn't it?"

Willoughby gulped and nodded.

"Then perhaps you could explain to me why you were drawing money to meet it from your clients' account at the London and Home Counties Bank. An account which, I cannot help reflecting, contains £20,000 of my money. You appreciate my interest in the matter?"

"What happened next?" said Jonas.

"Nothing much. He just pushed off. I'm terribly sorry about it. It was the coincidence of those two blighters turning up just when we were expecting Stukely."

"And the coincidence of me being away."

"Yes. There was that too. Do you think he's going to make trouble?"

"Yes," said Jonas. "I'm sure he's going to make trouble."

As a junior minister, Will Dylan had the use of a small room in the House which he shared with his three colleagues. At the moment it was occupied only by him and his agent, Mr. Clover.

Mr. Clover looked worried. He said, "It's difficult to put a finger on it, but I can smell trouble."

"Things seemed happy enough when I was up there last Monday."

"That's just when it seemed to start."

"What started?"

"Talk."

"Who's been talking?"

"Edgar Dyson, for one."

"Edgar's a hard-line Communist. He says what he's told to say."

"He's well thought of," said Mr. Clover. "Next to you, he's probably the most influential man in the district."

"As long as he's only the second most influential," said Will. He considered the matter. Clover was a good agent, a man who kept his ear to the ground. If he said that trouble was building up, it was a fact and would have to be faced.

"Can you give me some idea what line he's taking?"

"What he's saying is that he doesn't, personally, think you pocketed any of the union money."

"Kind of him."

"But he does think you ought to meet the accusation openly, now that it's been made, and not hide behind the technicalities of the law. They seem to have got hold of a slanted account of what happened in that Magistrates Court, and they don't like it much."

"They don't care a lot for magistrates in Todmoor," agreed Will. "What exactly does Dyson mean when he talks about meeting the accusation openly? Officially there's no accusation to meet. If Killey does succeed in getting out a summons, I shall defend it, of course."

"It's awkward."

"Until that happens, I think it's a case of least said, soonest mended."

A colleague shot into the room with a bundle of papers, saw Mr. Clover, said, "Sorry," dumped the papers on the table, and made for the door.

"It's all right, Mick," said Dylan. "We've finished." To Clover he said, "You say this trouble started up early last week?"

"That's right. After your visit."

"I wasn't the only visitor. Killey was up there too."

"I wasn't told about that," said Clover. "Do you think it was something he picked up while he was up there that started the trouble?"

"The only thing he picked up in Todmoor," said Dylan with a grin, "was a lovely black eye. Don't fret, Charlie. We've ridden out worse storms than this together."

It was eight o'clock that evening when he got back to Chiswick, and he was surprised to find Fred still up.

"You ought to have been in bed a long time ago," he said.

His wife came in from the kitchen. She said, "I told Fred to stay up until you came home. You've got to do something about it. I told him he'd be punished next time he did it."

130

"Did what?"

"He'll tell you," said Pauline and went out again, shutting the door behind her.

Fred looked at his father, and his father looked at Fred.

"Well?" said Will.

Fred said, "I diddun go to school."

"Why not?"

"I diddun want to."

At this point his own father would have said, "Get your pants down. You've earned yourself a belting."

He found himself incapable of saying it. Instead, in tones that were far from fierce, he said, "I thought you liked school. What's gone wrong?"

"They started saying things."

"You ought to be able to stand up to that. Call 'em names back again."

"It wasn't me they said things about," said Fred. "It was you. They said you'd been stealing money. They said it's in all the papers."

And he burst into tears.

"Aren't children beasts," said Will. Supper was over. Fred was tucked up in bed, unbeaten but fortified by much good advice. Pauline was sewing a patch into the elbow of a coat. She said, "Of course the papers never said any such thing."

"Papers don't have to say things. They've trained people to read between the lines. They've got a shorthand of their own. If you read that a clergyman has been charged with an offense 'involving choirboys,' you don't assume that he has been training the choir in shoplifting or conspiring with them to burn down the chapel, do you?"

Pauline said, "Sometimes I think we were happier before we had newspapers. Who can be ringing you up at this time of night?"

It was the Prime Minister's private secretary. He said that the

Prime Minister would be most obliged if Dylan could come around and have a word with him. Would he come by the private access through the Foreign Office and the garden of number eleven, as there was a deputation of Biafran ladies camped out in front of number ten and quite a number of pressmen with them.

"I'm sorry to drag you out on one of your few evenings at home," said the Prime Minister. "It must be particularly pleasant on the river on a night like this. The trouble is that my own day is parceled out for me into strict sections. When I want to conduct a little business of my own, it has to be squeezed in at odd hours."

Dylan said he quite understood. Typical of the old man to indicate, indirectly, that he was sufficiently interested in you to know where you lived. He sounded friendly. Dangerous to build on it. The hand behind his back could hold a bouquet or an axe. You wouldn't know until he brought it out.

"One of the reasons I didn't want the press to see you, and certain other people coming in, was that they might have jumped to conclusions. Which, in this case, would have been perfectly correct. I've made up my mind to go to the Country in October. The precise date hasn't been fixed, but it'll be in the first two weeks of the month. I never embark on a general election without assuming"—the Prime Minister switched on his famous smile—"that I'm going to win it. I make my plans on this assumption, and I make them well in advance. In the next government which I form I want to offer you the Ministry of Labor."

When Christopher Martingale got to the Law Society on Friday morning, there was a note on his desk from Laurence Fairbrass asking him to look in, but when he got to Laurence's office it was empty. As he was wondering what to do, Laurence came in with a letter in his hand.

"I've been having a word with Tom," he said. "It's Killey again. Have a look at this."

The letter was handwritten, on Club notepaper, and covered two pages. It was signed A. R. Stukely. Christopher read it carefully.

"According to this it wasn't Killey who drew the check," he said. "It was his partner."

"Willoughby's a salaried partner. In fact, an employee. Killey's responsible for anything he does. You know that perfectly well."

Christopher knew it perfectly well.

"What do you want me to do?"

"We shall have to look into it. You've got the file. You'd better start the ball rolling."

When a complaint is made against a solicitor, the Professional Purposes Section of the Law Society has to make a preliminary investigation. If it seems to be a prima facie case, it makes a report to the Council, who have to decide whether to prosecute or not. They don't try the case themselves. It comes before the Disciplinary Committee, which is a separate statutory body, set up by the Lord Chancellor. Most cases are fairly cut and dried and don't attract a lot of attention. The offender is reprimanded, or fined, or struck off, and there is a note in the *Gazette* and that's the end of the matter.

"Write him the usual letter," said Laurence. "And it mightn't be a bad idea if you went down to see him. You know him better than most. He's more likely to talk to you than to a stranger."

"If I'm any judge of Jonas' character," said Christopher, "he won't talk to me, or anyone. He'll sulk in his tent and defy us to do our worst."

At this point one of the porters appeared. He said, "There's a Mr. Killey asking for you, sir." Laurence grinned and said, "I'll leave him to you."

The first thing Christopher noticed about Jonas was the bruise on his face. It was more than a mere black eye. It had highlighted the whole of the left-hand side of his face in shades of blue-black, purple, and yellow.

"Have you been in a fight?" he said.

"I was assaulted by a pack of louts," said Jonas. "But that's not what I've come to talk about. Or not directly." He spotted the letter. "Is that from that man who calls himself Stukely?" Before Christopher could stop him, he had picked it up and started reading it.

"I don't think you're meant to see that. It's a privileged communication."

"It's a pack of lies," said Jonas when he had finished reading it.

"You mean it didn't happen?"

"The sequence of events it describes did actually occur."

"Then how can it be a pack of lies?"

"If you would be good enough to allow me to state the case,

134

without adopting an attitude of officialdom simply because you happen to be sitting behind an official desk, I'll do my humble best to give you the facts."

"Carry on," said Christopher. He had known Jonas too long to allow himself to be nettled. At the end he said, "So you're telling me it was a put-up job."

"If you were listening, that will be the impression you will have obtained, I should imagine."

"There are one or two coincidences," Christopher agreed. "But coincidences do happen in real life. If the thing was planned, how do you suppose they did it? Weren't they a bit lucky in their timing?"

"There was no luck about it. My office telephone had been tapped. They knew I had left to look after my mother."

"But how were they to know it was going to happen at all? Or was that a put-up job too?"

"Of course. It was probably the same two men. They had plenty of time to get down to Wimbledon."

"But why—"

"Why what?"

"Why should anyone go to all that trouble to rig up a case against you. Trouble *and* expense. You say Mr. Stukely actually deposited £20,000 in your client account. It's a lot of money."

"I imagine the government can find £20,000 if it suits its purpose."

Christopher stared at him.

"Are you serious?" he said at last.

"I have not come here to make jokes. Or to have my word doubted. The Law Society exists to protect the interests of solicitors. You agree with that, I imagine."

"It's one of its functions."

"It's what I pay my subscription for. A subscription, incidentally, which helps to pay *your* salary. Let us be clear about this. I am not asking for a favor. I have the right to be helped, and I propose to see that I get it."

But Christopher was still trying to grapple with the preposterous idea. He said, "I simply don't believe that governments behave like that."

"What you are prepared to believe is a matter of little interest to me," said Jonas. "If you don't wish to help, perhaps you will arrange for me to see someone who will."

"What exactly do you want us to do?"

"This man Stukely must be investigated. He's clearly a professional *agent provocateur.*"

"I don't think we're geared for that sort of job. And anyway, we're meant to be investigating *your* conduct. Not his."

"I can see that it's useless talking to you."

"When a solicitor's accused of professional misconduct, he usually gets another firm to represent him. Why don't you do that? Lambard would be glad to help."

"I have already approached Mr. Lambard, and he made it quite clear that he was not interested."

"Already?"

"Not on this precise point, no. On a connected matter."

"Try him again," Christopher said. "This is different. You were a member of his staff. He'll certainly do it."

"Of all the solicitors in London," said Jonas, "I can think of few less suitable. What we are up against here is the Establishment, of which he is himself a member. Now, if you've quite finished evading the issue, perhaps you'll answer my question. Are you prepared to help, or not?"

"I'll have a word with my boss," Christopher said unhappily.

Laurence Fairbrass said, "Get the file up and prepare a preliminary report. It'll have to go up to Tom. I didn't want to bother him, because he's up to the neck with this Law Revision Committee, but we'll have to let him know what's happening."

"You don't really believe that there's anything in this—in this theory of Killey's."

"I don't believe anything until it's proved," said Laurence.

Christopher went to look for old Reiss. He was one of the characters of the Society. No one knew how old he was. By an oversight the authorities had forgotten to put the usual clause in his service contract about retirement at sixty-five, and he had simply refused to go. He said that as long as he did his job, his age was a matter for him alone. Anyway, he'd organized his filing system so that no one else could understand it.

He lived in a hutch down in the rambling basement of strong-rooms and cellars which stretch from Bell Yard to Chancery Lane. When Christopher told him what he wanted, Reiss consulted a battered exercise book which was filled with entries in his own illegible handwriting, and he led the way along the passage, jingling a bunch of keys like a warder in the Château d'If. He paused outside one of the doors. "You know what I've got in there? Forty-five years of professional misconduct. Six hundred and sixty-two cases. This one will be six hundred and sixty-three."

"Not yet," Christopher said. "It isn't proved yet."

"Tell me about it," said Reiss. He had found the folder he wanted in a large cupboard farther along the passage.

When they got back to his den, Christopher gave him the outline of the case. Reiss liked to be kept in the picture. He listened, nodding his head, with his spectacles on the end of his nose.

"This man Stukely. He'd only been Mr. Killey's client for a couple of weeks?"

"Less than that."

"And he left £20,000 with his firm. After just one visit."

"That's right. Why?"

"Funny sort of way to carry on," said Reiss.

It was after tea when Reiss appeared in Christopher's office.

He had a yellowing dog-eared folder in his hand and a smug expression on his face. He said, "Like I was saying, it was funny."

"What was funny, Reiss?"

"Him being a new client. The one you were talking about."

Christopher understood quite well what he meant by that. Causes of dissatisfaction between solicitor and client are normally of slower growth.

"So I got out this one. I thought you might like to have a look at it."

The file was twenty-five years old and dealt with a period not long after the war. A solicitor called Palmer had apparently got it into his head that the Minister of War Production had promised his father half a million pounds for an invention which looked, from the sparse details in the file, to be remarkably like radar. Christopher knew very little about radar. He seemed to remember that it had been invented in the first years of the war. Mr. Palmer, however, claimed that his father had already invented it in the 1920s. He had not patented it, but there were family documents to prove it.

When the Minister rejected his claim, Mr. Palmer had embarked on a campaign of persecution. He had written articles and letters to the papers which must have put him, and them, in danger of an action for libel. Then he had turned to the courts and instituted three separate actions against the Minister personally. One for breach of contract, one for conversion, and a third, for good measure, for slander.

At this point, before any of the actions could be heard, he had assaulted a client. There was a statement by the client, a Mr. Sempill, in the file. He was a new client, and it was on the occasion of his first visit that he had incautiously made some favorable comment about the minister concerned, whereupon, according to him, Mr. Palmer had got up and hit him repeatedly in the face, causing severe lacerations. Mr. Sempill had taken out a summons for assault.

In court Mr. Palmer had given *his* version of the matter. He said that Mr. Sempill had come into his office and simply started to insult him. He had used vile and offensive language about Mr.

Palmer, Mr. Palmer's wife, and Mr. Palmer's family. When Mr. Palmer could stand no more of this, he had tried to push him from the room, and a struggle had ensued in which, he admitted, blows had been struck.

When the magistrate inquired why Mr. Sempill, a complete stranger, should have behaved in such an incredible way, Mr. Palmer could only suggest that he was a minion of the Minister of War Production, about whom he had added a few slanderous comments. This had not gone down well with the magistrate. Result: a sharp dressing-down and bound over to keep the peace.

Unfortunately this was something Mr. Palmer seemed unable to do. Two months later, encountering Mr. Sempill again, he had again struck him. The details of this second assault were obscure, because before it came to court Mr. Palmer had been found in his own garage, lying behind his car with the engine churning out carbon monoxide. Verdict: suicide while the balance of his mind was disturbed.

Christopher closed the file and said to Reiss, who had been sitting there watching him, "It's an odd story, and Sempill was certainly a new client. But apart from that there isn't a particle of similarity between the two cases."

"That's right," said Reiss. "Just him being a new client. But it wasn't this one I was thinking about. Not really. I got it out to show you, because I knew where I could lay my hands on it. The other one's very similar. Very similar indeed, as I recollect it. And not so long ago, either."

"Then let's have a look at it."

"We can't."

"Why not?"

"Because I've forgotten the name. I know about when it was. Say ten years ago, give or take a year either side."

"So?"

"What I thought was, why don't we have a look for it, you and me. It won't take more than a day. We could do it tomorrow."

"Tomorrow's Saturday. The place will be shut."

"I've got a key."

Christopher thought about it. Chiefly he thought about what Mutt would say. What she did say, when he put it to her, was that if there was any chance it might help Jonas, he ought to do it. So up he came.

Christopher had never realized before in what curious ways solicitors could misbehave. It wasn't just a matter of embezzling their clients' money. Cases of this sort were rare. Surprisingly so, when you consider the trusting way in which clients hand over large sums of money to them. Most of the financial cases were examples of reasonably honest muddle. The Solicitors' Account and Audit Rules are complex, and while big firms with specialist staff can cope with them, an overworked one-man solicitor must find them full of traps.

There were cases of overcharging, and of the equally serious offense of undercharging. There were solicitors who had practiced without the formality of obtaining a practicing certificate. There were others who had conducted lucrative businesses without being qualified at all, usually by attaching themselves to an elderly and incompetent solicitor and using him as a front, in the manner of Uriah Heep.

There were a number of ingenious cases of unprofessional advertising. One man, not content with having a nameplate beside his entrance which was almost as big as the door itself, had put a further notice at the corner of the street with a painted hand pointing down it and the name of his firm inscribed in gold letters on the index finger. Another had adopted the simpler course of leaving his professional card tucked into the corner of the mirror in first-class railway carriages.

When they broke for lunch at one o'clock, Reiss grumbled, "If you read 'em all right through, we'll never get done. Just keep your eyes open for a new client who makes a complaint about money coming out of the wrong account."

"But they're so interesting," Christopher said. "Did you know that one man inserted more than fifty advertisements in the papers for fictitious missing persons? A lot of the people who turned up were so impressed by his business methods that they became his clients on the spot."

"That's nothing," said Reiss. "There was a man just after the war who put his receptionist behind a plate-glass window in the Strand. Smashing girl too. You'd be surprised the clients *he* got."

It was late in the afternoon when Reiss gave a grunt of satisfaction. "Got it," he said. "It was longer ago than I thought. Nearly twelve years. Let's take it back to my room, then we can both look at it."

It wasn't a nice case. The plaintiff was a captain in the R.A.S.C. who was claiming a large sum of money from a prominent government back-bencher. Even Christopher, who took very little interest in politics, recognized the name. He was not only an M.P., he was a man of great wealth who was known to have contributed very heavily to party funds, and he was a considerable public figure: a man who opened boys' clubs, attended first nights, sponsored good causes, and employed a first-class press agent to ensure that the public noticed him doing it. On paper the claim by the R.A.S.C. captain was ridiculous. It was so flimsy that it seemed surprising that he should have troubled to bring the action at all. The solicitor he employed had apparently thought otherwise. He was confident that the case would be settled before it came to court, and the reason for his confidence was that he had got hold of a number of letters written by a young soldier in the captain's own company to the back-bencher and had so organized the pleadings that these letters would be produced and referred to at the hearing. There were copies of the letters in the file.

"Wouldn't want *them* read out in court," said Reiss.

Christopher agreed. They might not have led to a criminal

charge, but they would certainly have meant the end of public life for the back-bencher. It was at this point that a Mr. Herman had called on the solicitor. *And, before Christopher's fascinated and incredulous eyes, the Stukely story unrolled, alike in all essential particulars.* The projected trust, the deposit of money, the arrival of the debt collectors, the dispatch of a messenger to the bank, the fortuitous arrival of Mr. Herman. The only variation in this case was that it was the solicitor himself, and not his junior partner, who was led into the trap.

The story had ended with the solicitor being struck off the rolls and the captain, for reasons which were not clear, dropping the case altogether. Christopher read it through twice, conscious of old Reiss's bright and inquiring eye on him.

"Odd sort of business, don't you think?" he said.

"It's more than odd."

"Could be a coincidence, of course."

"It could be. I'll keep the file out. And I don't think you'd better say much about this, just for the moment."

"Lucky you mentioned it," said Reiss with a grin. "I had thought of walking down the street and selling it to the *News of the World.*"

As soon as he got home, Christopher disregarded the good advice he had given Reiss and told Mutt the whole story. She listened with her head on one side and, for once, without interrupting. At the end she said, "So that means that Jonas was framed."

"It could have been a coincidence."

"Nonsense. Of course it isn't a coincidence. And you don't think it is either."

"But who—"

"What you're boggling at," said his wife calmly, "is the thought that the people in power could behave like a bunch of crooks. That's because you're a man. Men always tend to support the Establishment. I don't boggle. I think that governments are just as crooked as ordinary crooks. The difference is they're not as clever at it. They're amateurs."

Although Christopher tried to reopen the subject, that was all she would say about it, until much later that night. When he was just turning over and drifting off to sleep, she said, "I suppose you'll pass that file up to Laurence, or Tom Buller."

"I shall have to do that."

"And as far as you're concerned, that'll be the end of it. You won't be involved any more."

"I don't suppose I shall," Christopher said. "Why?"

Mutt put one bare arm around his neck and said, "I don't want you to get involved. It's a dirty business. Much too dirty for a nice simple person like you."

"That's what you think. I'm not really simple. I'm devious, cunning, and unprincipled."

"Machiavelli in person," said Mutt and kissed him tenderly.

Christopher hadn't realized until then how worried she was.

It was midday on Monday when Christopher got the summons he had been expecting and went along to Tom Buller's room. Laurence was there, and the report of the Herman case was on the desk. If Christopher thought he was going to be commended for initiative he was rapidly undeceived.

Tom said, "How did this report come to light?"

"It was Reiss."

"What had Reiss got to do with it?"

"He spotted the fact that the complaint had been made by a brand-new client. He thought he remembered a similar case, and we looked it up."

"Do you mean to say that you discussed a disciplinary complaint with our muniments clerk?"

"I didn't discuss it," Christopher said unhappily. "Reiss always reads the papers before he puts them away."

"He may read the papers after the matter is concluded. He has absolutely no right to see them when the matter is still sub judice."

Christopher had nothing to say to that. In fact, as they both knew, Reiss was a model of discretion, and no possible harm had been done. But it was not the moment to say so.

After glowering at Christopher for a few moments, Tom picked up the papers again and read them through in silence. Then he said in a slightly more reasonable voice, "In the course of this unauthorized investigation of yours did you happen to find any more cases like it?"

"There was one. It could have been a put-up job. But it was a good time ago and the circumstances were rather different."

He told him about the Palmer case.

Tom said to Laurence, "Then I'd better see those papers too." And to Christopher, "Please get hold of Mr. Lambard and ask him if he'd be good enough to come round here this afternoon."

"Any particular time?"

"Any time that suits him. I'll cancel any appointment I've got."

In the passage outside, Laurence squeezed Christopher's arm affectionately and said, "Stop looking like a stuffed owl."

"Was I?"

"I thought you were going to burst into tears."

"Why did he have to take it out on me?"

"In the old days," said Laurence, "great men used to have a special boy they could kick on the bottom when things went wrong. It was a highly paid post."

"Must have been highly skilled too," Christopher said. "Was he really angry?"

"I've known Tom for a long time," said Laurence. "And I've never known him as angry as he was when he saw those papers. If it's any comfort to you, he spent a quarter of an hour slanging me before you got there."

"It's a fantastic story," said Lambard. "Could be a coincidence."

"I don't think it's a coincidence."

"If you're right, you realize what it means?"

145

"It means there's an agency of the government which is prepared to break the law in order to protect its own people, if they're important enough."

"Does it surprise you?"

"I'm not surprised," said Buller. "But I'm shocked. And I'm unclear what I ought to do about it."

"Do you think the case is proved?"

"Proved? Legally proved, you mean? No. But I've made a few inquiries. I telephoned those builders. All they could tell me was that a man had come along and bought their debt at a small discount."

"There are firms who do that."

"Certainly. The man said he worked for an outfit called Raven Service. We know most of the regular debt-collecting agencies, and they all know each other. None of them seem to have heard of a Raven Service, and the name doesn't appear on the Register of Business Names."

"It could be a new firm."

"Yes," said Buller. "It could be."

The two men sat in silence, each busy with his own thoughts. Buller said at last, "There's one significant difference. In the earlier case they operated on the solicitor himself. I knew the man. We had quite a dossier on him here already. He was a bad 'un. Sooner or later he was going to get struck off anyway. I don't suppose he thought twice about paying a private bill out of his clients' money. He'd probably done it often enough before. It was just that until Herman came along we hadn't been able to prove it. With Killey it was quite different. He'd never have fallen for it. He's rigidly honest and far too experienced. If it was to work, they had to get him out of the way and operate on his assistant, who was young enough and green enough to be bounced."

"And that's the reason for that business with his old mother."

"Yes."

"A bit risky, wasn't it? Suppose the friendly neighbor *hadn't* rung up? Or suppose he hadn't been worried enough to go rushing off?"

"There was no risk involved. They had his telephone tapped."

Lambard opened his mouth as if to say something, and then changed his mind and shut it again. There was another long silence, broken by a young man who opened the door, saw Lambard, and said, "Sorry. I didn't know you had a visitor."

"If you can't read the word 'Engaged' on my door," said Buller in tones of cold hatred, "there's no future for you in this Society."

The young man gasped once and disappeared.

Lambard said, "I imagine you're not going to let the matter rest here."

"I can't do that."

"What do you propose to do about it?"

"When a solicitor is accused of professional misconduct, he normally gets another solicitor to represent him. That involves looking into all the circumstances of the case. It would be natural to investigate any promising line of defense."

"And you want me to do that?"

"I can think of no one I'd rather entrust it to."

"Good of you to say so," said Lambard. "But in this case it's not you who's doing the entrusting. It's Killey. And of all the firms in London, I'm probably the last one he'd care to approach."

"Why? He knows you well."

"He came to me last week and asked me to help him with an appeal in his case against Dylan. From what I know of his character, I guess it must have cost him a considerable effort to come at all. He's not a man who likes asking for help."

"And you turned him down."

"I thought he was flogging a dead horse, and I told him so."

"But this is quite different."

"Quite different," agreed Lambard.

"Will you at least ask him?"

There was such a long silence that Lambard seemed to have been thinking about something different. In the end he said abruptly, "I'll have to think about it. I'll give you my answer in the morning."

When he got back to his office, Lambard telephoned his wife. He said, "It's much too hot in London. I'm going to get away early and come home for the night."

"You won't see a lot of me," said his wife. "It's Women's Institute Night."

"Give them a miss for once."

"I can't do that. I'm introducing the speaker. A very interesting woman who's spent most of her life in Fiji."

"All right," said Lambard. "As a matter of fact I have got something I've got to think over. A quiet evening at home is just what the doctor ordered."

"Penny will look after you."

"Is she home?"

"She came back last night. She's got a week off."

"Splendid," said Lambard. Of all his family, he found her the easiest to talk to.

After dinner, sitting out on the lawn under the cedar of Lebanon in the companionable dusk, he told her the whole story. She was a good listener. It wasn't until right at the end that she said, "I rather liked Mr. Killey."

"I'd no idea you knew him."

"I met him at the hospital when he came down to ask after his mother. That was a swinish thing to do, deliberately upsetting an old lady like that. Do you realize it might easily have killed her? Maybe it will."

"Was she as bad as that?"

"We didn't tell Jonas, but as a matter of fact her heart is getting very tired. It might stop working at any moment."

"Kinder than cancer," said her father, who was old enough to start thinking of such things.

"What are you going to do. About Killey?"

"I don't know. Even if I wanted to help him, I don't know that he'd have me."

"He's a prickly character," agreed Penny. "If you wanted to help him, you'd have to set about it very tactfully." She thought for a moment. "What you'd have to say is that you'd refused his first offer because you were too busy, but now one of your— What do you call them—cases?"

"Matters."

"One of your matters has fallen through, and you'd like to handle this, if he'd let you, because it's technically very interesting."

"The mandamus, you mean?"

"That's right. And if he agreed, he'd be bound to mention the other thing, and you'd say, if you were doing one you might just as well handle both of them."

"You're in the wrong job," said her father. "You ought to be in the diplomatic service. The one thing you haven't told me is whether you think I ought to do it at all."

"Personal opinion?"

"Personal opinion."

"I think you were right to say no the first time. I think you'd be wrong to say no to this. You've got to stand up for your own gang."

"I'm afraid you're right," said Lambard. He sighed deeply. "It's going to be a lot of hard and ungrateful work. I'd go into it with much more enthusiasm if I could be absolutely convinced that we weren't imagining things. It seems monstrous, somehow, that the men we've entrusted with the government of this country—men who I should have said were perfectly decent people—should have done a thing like this."

"It doesn't surprise me a lot," said Penny. "People who've got hold of power will do almost anything to keep it."

Lambard said, "I'm going to tell you something which you mustn't tell anyone else. Particularly your mother. Bill Sexton

149

told me this morning that I'm to be offered a knighthood. They made the approach through him because they wanted details of my professional career. He thought it was the work I did on the Restrictive Practices Commission."

"I expect that's right, isn't it?"

"I'm beginning to wonder. If they had Killey watched, they'll have known he came to see me. And they'd guess I'd be asked to help him. I was the natural person. It crossed my mind that this might be a way of choking me off. There's nothing official about the offer yet. It could easily be withdrawn."

"If that's right," said Penelope, "There's no doubt at all what you ought to do. Weigh right in and hit the bastards where it hurts."

As was his habit, Mr. Gazelee had come to court early, entering by the private door at the back of the building. He had spent some time in his room studying his papers and trying without success to complete the awkward left-hand bottom corner of the *Times* crossword.

At ten o'clock, to the accompaniment of the usher's resonant "Stand please," he stalked into the courtroom from behind the podium and stood for a moment surveying the court. It seemed to be unusually crowded. The back of the room was normally almost empty. Now there were twenty or more men in it. The press benches were full too, and latecomers had edged their way onto the seats normally reserved for solicitors.

As far as he knew, there was nothing on the list that morning to justify such interest. No extradition, no sex, no trade unions. The normal routine of motoring offenses and minor assaults. A young drunk coming up for sentencing. As he was on the point of sitting down, he received a second surprise, almost a shock. On the long front bench drooped a figure he recognized. Counsel rarely appeared in his court; leading counsel of the eminence of Marcus Hoyle very rarely indeed.

Mr. Gazelee sniffed. He could sense a certain tension in the air. He looked down at his clerk, who said, "Number one, case adjourned from last Tuesday. The police against Mauger."

The shirtsleeved policeman shouted, "Number one," and Patrick, who had been waiting for his cue, advanced, and took post in front of the iron-railed dock. He was a very different figure from the soiled and disheveled creature who had faced the court eight days before.

Mr. Gazelee looked at him over his glasses for a moment, as if trying to identify him, then glanced down at his notes and said, "I adjourned this matter to see whether the police could contact the girl who was referred to in evidence. Might I inquire whether you have been successful?"

The inspector rose smartly to his feet, said, "I am afraid not, sir," and subsided.

"In that case," said the magistrate, "all that remains for me to do is to bring this matter to a conclusion."

"If you please," said Marcus Hoyle. He had unfolded himself and now stood, his head thrust forward, his white hair falling over one eye, and looking, thought Patrick, like a heron surveying a promising fish pond.

"Well, Mr. Hoyle?"

"I should like permission to call one further witness."

"I'm afraid you're too late. The case was closed on the previous occasion."

"With respect, I can hardly think that was so. The case was adjourned for further possible evidence on behalf of the prosecution. I understand that they have not been successful. I, on the other hand, have a witness who can give us an independent account of what transpired."

Mr. Gazelee hesitated. He had faced packed courts before in many of his cases, but this crowd puzzled him. Though herded together to a point almost of discomfort, they were perfectly silent and showing no signs of restlessness. They gave him the impression that they were waiting for a cue.

He said, "Very well, Mr. Hoyle."

"Then I will call Mr. Goodbody."

A small man with a whispy red beard who had been sitting on a chair near the side door of the court sprang to his feet and climbed into the witness box. He snatched the testament out of the usher's hand, repeated the oath without waiting to be prompted, turned toward counsel and said, "My name is Maximilian Goodbody and I reside at 23 Cremona Terrace, North 16."

Marcus Hoyle said with a smile, "It's more usual to wait until you're asked, Mr. Goodbody. However, that information has now been recorded. Could we come at once to the night of Monday July eighth?"

"By all means. At approximately two A.M. on the early morning of Tuesday July ninth I was sitting on a bench which commands a view of the junction of Rickaby Street and Corfield Gardens. I had been unable to sleep and was taking the air. Approximately twenty minutes later I observed a young lady who approached from the direction of Holborn and seated herself on the sand bin up against the railings of Corfield Gardens. She did not observe me. Approximately five minutes later—"

"I'm afraid, Mr. Goodbody, that you'll have to go a little slower. You're leaving the shorthand writer behind."

"You're leaving us all behind," said Mr. Gazelee. "Wouldn't it be better, Mr. Hoyle, if you proceeded by question and answer."

"If it will assist the court. Tell us then, Mr. Goodbody, what happened next?"

"The next thing was that the accused arrived and started talking to the girl."

"Was it your impression that he was annoying her?"

"Certainly not. They were talking and laughing together in a very friendly way."

"I see. And then?"

"Then," said Mr. Goodbody, "two other men appeared on the scene. They came from the same direction as the accused, and

153

I gained the impression that they had been following him."

The inspector looked up sharply, scribbled a note, and passed it to the policeman standing near his box.

"Do you see these men in court?"

"I do."

"Perhaps you would point them out to us."

"The young one with the black mustache over there. And the older one with the bald head sitting beside him."

"And what happened next?"

"The two men approached the accused and the girl. I could not hear what was said. I think they were ordering her to go away, because she put her shoes on—I forgot to say she had slipped them off when sitting down on the sand bin—and started to go away. As soon as she had gone, the older of the two men stepped up to the accused, said something in a loud voice, and struck him."

"Had the accused said or done anything?"

"No."

"Then it was an unprovoked blow?"

"Absolutely unprovoked. A very savage blow indeed."

A note was passed from Sergeant McGillivray to the inspector, who looked at it, smiled briefly, and added it to his papers. If Marcus Hoyle noticed these exchanges, he disregarded them. He said, "And then, Mr. Goodbody?"

"The accused fell to the ground and the younger of the two men kicked him. He kicked him more than once as he lay on the ground."

"And then?"

"Then a car drove up. The accused was dragged into it, and the car went off."

"Thank you," said Marcus Hoyle.

The inspector said, "I understand, Mr. Goodbody, that you are a regular attender at this court."

"I am."

"And that you were here last Tuesday when the accused was giving us his account of what occurred?"

"I was."

"So that you would have heard on that occasion most of the facts which you have related to us this morning?"

"I certainly heard what he said. And as I had been present myself, I thought it my duty to come forward."

The inspector considered the reply, looked speculatively at the magistrate, and then said, "I have no further questions. But in view of some of the statements which have been made this morning, I ask leave to recall Sergeant McGillivray."

"You have no objection, Mr. Hoyle?"

"None at all," said Marcus Hoyle with the ghost of a smile.

"Very well."

"You have been sworn in these proceedings. There is no need to take the oath again. Now, Sergeant, on the night in question, was there a full moon?"

"No, sir. It was a new moon."

"How far away from this sand bin we have heard about is the nearest streetlamp?"

"Approximately twenty yards. Perhaps a little more."

"You heard the last witness mention a bench. Is there any bench in the vicinity?"

"I believe there is a bench inside Corfield Gardens."

"But the gardens are locked up at night?"

"That is so, sir."

"And if the witness had been sitting on that bench, would he have had a view of what was happening in the vicinity of the sand bin?"

"He might just have been able to see it if he stood on the bench."

"And would he have been able to recognize people at that distance, and in those circumstances?"

"I should have said it was quite impossible, sir."

"Thank you, Sergeant."

The sergeant made a half turn as if to leave the box, but the long figure of Marcus Hoyle was observed to be unfolding itself once more.

"Well, Sergeant," he said blandly, "so we meet again."

"I beg your pardon, sir?"

"I'm sure you haven't forgotten. I had the pleasure of cross-examining you in the case of the Police against Carbutt. The court did not believe your evidence, and Major Carbutt was acquitted."

The laugh which followed was so well synchronized that it might have come at the flick of a conductor's baton.

Mr. Gazelee beat once with his gavel on the desk in front of him, and the laughter ceased as suddenly as it had begun. He said, the anger thickening his words, "That was a most improper observation, Mr. Hoyle."

"I am always prepared to accept correction from the bench, sir, but I think that in this case I was within my rights."

"It was an absolutely irrelevant comment."

"It is some years since I studied the laws of evidence, but it was my impression—I stand ready to be corrected if I am wrong—that when the prosecution attack the character of the accused, their own witnesses are open to similar attack. In this case the prosecution has accused my client of drunkenness and, if not actual immorality, of boorish behavior to a young lady. I must surely be allowed to remind the witness that he committed perjury."

The word hung for a moment, and then the inspector leaped up. "I protest most emphatically, sir."

"Then I withdraw the word perjury," said Marcus Hoyle before Mr. Gazelee could speak. "It was, however, indisputable that in the case in question, had the sergeant been believed, the accused must have been convicted. It may have been, of course, that the bench did not think the witness was lying. They may merely have concluded that he was confused."

"I rule," said Mr. Gazelee, "that this line of questioning is entirely improper. I shall disregard it when coming to a conclusion."

"That is your undoubted privilege," said Marcus Hoyle. "Have you any more questions?"

"There are one or two other matters." Counsel referred to his notes. "When giving evidence in the original hearing you said that you and Detective Roper were on a routine patrol."

"Yes, sir."

"At two A.M.?"

"Yes, sir."

"And what particular routine calls for a sergeant and a detective of the Criminal Investigation Department to be walking the streets together at two o'clock in the morning?"

"There had been a number of cases of breaking and entering offices reported in that neighborhood."

"But surely, Sergeant, that is a matter for the uniformed branch."

"Normally that would be so, sir. But we had been instructed to assist them in this particular matter by keeping our eyes open."

"Then why did you not do so?"

"I beg your pardon?"

"In the course of your patrol you must have covered High Holborn."

"Yes."

"Where a case of breaking and entering an office occurred on that particular night. Well, Sergeant?"

"I believe that is so, sir."

"And was not noticed by you? Why was that? Was it because you were too engrossed in following the accused?"

"We were not following the accused, sir."

"You remember that you are giving evidence on oath, Sergeant."

"I do."

"And that if you lie on oath, you commit the crime of perjury."

Sergeant McGillivray, dark red in the face, suddenly said so loudly that it was almost a shout, "We—were—not—following —the—accused."

Marcus Hoyle looked down at his notes for a moment and said, "You stated in evidence that the accused was annoying this girl. What was he doing?"

The sudden switch disconcerted the witness, who said, "Well, he was—She was obviously upset."

"Yes. But what was he doing?"

"It was too dark to see exactly what he was doing."

"Could you hear what he said to her?"

"Not exactly."

"But, Sergeant, if you couldn't see what he was doing, or hear what he was saying, how could you tell that he was annoying and frightening her?"

"I could judge that from the girl's demeanor."

"And what was her demeanor?"

"She looked annoyed and frightened."

This seemed to amuse the audience. Mr. Gazelee rapped on his desk again and said, "If there is any more disturbance, I shall clear the court."

"You try it," said a voice from the back.

While Mr. Gazelee was trying to locate the speaker, he observed that counsel had resumed his seat.

He said, "If you have no questions, Inspector"—the inspector shook his head—"then it only remains for me to say that I reject entirely the evidence that the defense has produced at this late stage. I'm afraid I don't believe a word of it. And I reject and regret the attack which counsel has seen fit to make on these police officers. I find the accused guilty, and—"

"Shame," said a voice from the back of the court.

"Guilty, and I—"

"Why don't you listen to the evidence."

"Officer, remove that man."

The crowd at the back made no effort to obstruct the policeman, but neither did they help him. They simply stood. When the policeman had battled his way through them, he found himself faced by two or three impassive men, any of whom might have been the interrupter.

"Now then," he said, "which of you was it?"

"It was him," said Ben Thomas, indicating Syd Marvin.

"That's a lie," said Syd. "It was him."

"It wasn't either of them," said a third man. "It was me."

"Now then, Cecil," said Ben, "you mustn't go taking the blame."

These exchanges appeared to amuse the crowd, who applauded.

Mr. Gazelee, red in the face, said, "I'll have the court cleared." He signaled to the sergeant at the door, who could be heard shouting down the passage for reinforcements.

There was no trouble. The spectators filed out in perfect order. Marcus Hoyle, followed by his junior and his instructing solicitor, marched out with them.

It was in a courtroom occupied only by reporters and the police that Mr. Gazelee sentenced Patrick Mauger to a fine of fifty pounds with twenty pounds costs.

"A nice splash," said John Charles. He was studying the early afternoon editions of the evening papers spread out on his desk. "Q.C. ACCUSES POLICE." "UNPRECEDENTED SCENES IN COURT." "COUNSEL WALKS OUT." Good descriptive stuff. You won't get the real reactions until tomorrow morning. By that time people will have started to work out the implications."

"I expect we shall be helping them to do that," said Patrick. "Such is our duty."

"How did you unearth Maximilian Goodbody?"

"We didn't have to find him. He found us."

Patrick stared at him.

"Do you realize that we had more than a dozen people itching to give evidence. Three of them actually claimed to be the girl you talked to."

"But why wasn't I—?"

"We didn't need to bother you. One was in her middle fifties. One had a cleft palate and persecution mania. The third came from Tanzania. She wanted to protest against police brutality."

"Is everybody incurably mad?"

"It's a specialized form of madness," said Charles. "A desire to share in any limelight that happens to be going. Actresses and politicians occasionally suffer from it too."

"If you had all that talent, why did you pick on Goodbody? He was terribly unconvincing."

"We selected him *because* he was unconvincing."

"I don't understand."

"For maximum effect, we had to drag one of those policemen back into the witness box. The difficulty was that they had both concluded their evidence and there were no plausible grounds for recalling them. Hoyle reckoned that the only way of doing it was to put up a witness of our own who would be grossly insulting *and totally implausible*. Then they might be provoked into getting back into the box to shoot him down."

"Which they were."

"Which," agreed Charles with a grin, "they certainly were."

Jonas read the same reports on his way to Holborn to see Edward Lambard. He was not particularly interested in them. They merely confirmed his opinion that no policeman was to be relied on when he got into the witness box. He was more interested in a very small item which he found tucked away at the foot of the home news page. It was a report from Thorpe Common near Sheffield of a burglary at the house of a Mr. Mason, who was described as a retired businessman. The intruders had been interrupted by Mr. Mason's sister, who had attacked the intruders with remarkable courage—and with some success, since they had apparently left without taking anything of value.

Jonas was still pondering this account when he arrived at Lambard's office. He was in one of his less offensive moods and accepted Lambard's apologies and explanations graciously.

"Interesting," he said. "I agree. It should be technically interesting. Who are we briefing? A leader, of course. I may say that I now have an unexpected source of funds available."

"Fine," said Lambard. "For counsel I doubt if we could do better than Wilfred Cairns. I had a word with his clerk. He's free at the beginning of next week."

"Next week?"

"We had a bit of luck there. The appeal in the Wayland Steamship case folded up unexpectedly yesterday. It had been booked to run for at least a fortnight. The clerk of the lists has offered us Monday, with Tuesday if we need a second day. You realize that if this hadn't happened, we might have been held over until the autumn?"

"We shall have to move quickly."

"The main thing will be your affidavit. We'll get that roughed out now. And we shall have to put together the various exhibits. We had a bit of luck there. The *Watchman* has offered us a verbatim account of the original hearing. One of their men was in court and took down every word that was said. We'll take an affidavit from him and exhibit the statement to it. The other side will kick, but we would manage to slip it in that way."

"I also have some news for you," said Jonas. "You may remember that one of the main points I was criticized for was producing copies of documents and not originals. Particularly that last set of ACAT accounts."

"I mentioned it to Cairns. He thinks we might persuade the court to accept copies."

"There's no need," said Jonas. "I now have the original." He produced from his brief case a green-covered set of accounts and laid them on the table.

Lambard looked at him speculatively and said, "Would it be better if I didn't inquire how these came into your possession?"

"So far as I'm concerned, I have nothing to hide. They arrived by post this morning."

"With no covering letter?"

"There was a typed card with them. It said, 'From a well-wisher.' Nothing else."

Lambard thought about it. He said, "It may be a bit tricky to produce them at this stage. We'll have to leave the decision to Cairns. I'll fix a conference for after court on Friday. That should just give us time to get ready."

The editorial which appeared in the *Watchman* on Thursday morning was headlined "The Mind of Mr. Gazelee." It was unmistakably the editor's own work.

John Charles' friends used to say that he would have made a successful political bishop. His enemies called him a confidence trickster. There was justice in both verdicts.

It is true that his more solemn utterances had the clang of the pulpit about them, and he had a knack of framing platitudes so that they sounded like deep and original truths. But what he excelled in was construction. Like a crafty boxer he kept his opponent's eye fixed on his right hand, and then hit him hard and suddenly with his left.

The article started by summarizing the case of the Police against Mauger. It did not disguise the fact that the *Watchman* had a personal interest in the matter, Mauger being one of their own men. "Knowing Mauger as we do enables us to judge more justly than an outsider of the extreme unlikeliness of the prosecution case. When the verdict of a magistrate is greeted with open dissent from the public in the body of the court, it is not always the public who are wrong. Surely we are entitled to ask" —*here the flutes sounded a new motif*—"what made Mr. Gazelee change his mind? For change it he certainly did. A week ago he decided that the evidence against Mauger was not conclusive. The evidence of the police was contradicted by the accused. And so, very reasonably, Mr. Gazelee asked for outside evidence to support one or the other of the versions he had heard. He wanted the girl in the case to come forward. If she supported the police, that was an end of the matter. What happened?" *Pause for a rumbling of drums.* "A witness appeared. But he did *not* support the police. He entirely corroborated the version of the accused. Yet, curiously enough, Mr. Gazelee now found the charge proved. What made him change his mind? What influence had brought him to so radical a change in his views?" *A menacing whisper from the strings on*

163

the word "influence." "Is it too farfetched to suggest that Mr. Gazelee's attention may have been drawn to a recent article written in this paper by the accused? An article in which the accused had the temerity to criticize, by implication, a decision of Mr. Gazelee's brother magistrate in the West London Court. Are our magistrates so resentful of criticism that an arrow aimed at one of them will wound one of his fellows by proxy? We cannot, of course, know what curious considerations influenced Mr. Gazelee. The devil himself, said an eminent lawyer, knoweth not the mind of man. But this much is clear." *Full orchestra.* "An injustice has been done. It must be put right. We call upon the Home Secretary to institute an independent inquiry into the matter. Justice must not only be done, it must be seen to be done." *Bang. Bang.*

The editors of rival journals in and around Fleet Street read this remarkable effusion with attention. "So that's what the old devil's up to," they said. "Some link between the Dylan case and this one? Police being used as government pawns? Not very probable. But suppose it were true? Political dynamite. Particularly with an election in the offing. But dynamite mishandled, as we all know, can blow up in the face of its user."

The national press decided to follow the hunt, but to follow it for the moment at a safe distance.

The papers which supported the government deplored another attempt to blacken the reputation of the finest police force in the world, and deplored even more a personal attack on a magistrate who, being a public official, could not defend himself.

The opposition papers were not so sure. They had studied once again the reports on the original hearing. They reminded themselves at some length that they were debarred from comment on the case, since it was under appeal and therefore sub judice (thus, in fact, commenting on it both fully and safely). But as a general principle, they said, and quite apart from specific instances, *was* it right, in the case of a man seeking a remedy against a member of the government, that the availability of that remedy should depend upon a magistrate. After all, a magistrate had not got the same absolute safety from removal as a High Court judge. It was, of course, true that a magistrate's decision could be tested by the process of mandamus in the High Court, but this was a complicated and expensive procedure. Surely it would be better, *if any doubt at all existed,* for the summons to be granted, so that the matter could be tried by due process of law.

The *Times* refrained from comment.

At eleven o'clock that morning the Director of Public Prosecutions left his office in Buckingham Gate. The sun was already very hot. He had both windows of his official car wound down, and he told the chauffeur to drive slowly. The truth was, he wanted time to think. The car proceeded at a sedate pace down Birdcage Walk, around Parliament Square, and past the façade of both Houses before it turned in at the Lord Chancellor's gate. The policeman on duty, who was expecting him, pressed the button which raised the automatic barrier. The big car slid through the archway with not more than a foot to spare on either side, crossed the small courtyard, and came to rest in the larger courtyard beyond.

As the Director got out, the young barrister who was the Lord Chancellor's private secretary hurried out to meet him. Together they entered the lift. (It had been installed by the last chancellor but four, a man of more weight in his body than his judgments.) Alighting at the second floor, they walked along a passageway from both walls of which previous chancellors looked down their noses at them, and they came finally to the large light room overlooking the Thames on one side and Black Rod's garden on the other, which is the inmost sanctum of the British legal system.

The Lord Chancellor who got up to greet the Director was a short man with a face like a prize fighter. He said, "You know why I've sent for you?"

"Not difficult to guess."

"Have you read the article?"

"Certainly. It was also sent to me separately, by three members of Parliament, one High Court judge and the chairman of the Metropolitan Magistrates Association."

"Do you think it's actionable?"

"Defamatory, you mean?"

"Yes."

"No, I don't. I think a jury would almost certainly hold it to be fair comment on a matter of public interest."

"Do you think it's contempt of court?"

"That's much more difficult to answer. If the hearing had been committal proceedings, to be followed by a jury trial, one would assume that the jury would read the article and would be influenced by it. In which case, in my view, it would constitute contempt."

"So?"

"But this is rather different, isn't it?"

"Why?"

"The next step in this case is a hearing in the Court of Appeal. Can one suppose that three experienced judges are going to be influenced in their decision by a newspaper article?"

"Surely the test is objective, not subjective. It doesn't matter who is going to read the article. If it comments on a case while it's proceeding, in a way which could affect the mind of a reader, that is contempt of court."

"That may have been so once. I'm afraid it's not the way the courts apply it now. In recent cases—"

"You're thinking of the distillers."

"Among others."

"And you're advising me that a charge of contempt would not stand up."

The Director considered his answer very carefully. He tried not to let the fact that he disliked the Chancellor influence him. He said, "I think it's a borderline case. You might secure a verdict at the end of the day. Part of the article is a serious and personal attack on the magistrate who heard the application. And he is the magistrate to whom the application will have to be referred back if the action in the High Court succeeds. That must be objectionable."

When the Director paused, the Chancellor said, "I was sure that sentence was going to end with the word 'but.' You think a charge would lie, but—"

"You want my personal opinion?"

"That is why I interrupted your busy morning, Director."

"I think it would be inadvisable."

"Why do you think that?"

"Because it would appear to the public that the judiciary were lending themselves to a cover-up operation by the executive."

That produced a very long silence indeed. Then the Chancellor said, in a voice which tinkled with ice, "Well, I asked for your personal opinion, and you've certainly given it to me. You say, 'people might think.' You wouldn't, I take it, subscribe to the view yourself."

"If you mean," said the Director, "do I think that those two policemen were deliberately set onto Mauger to discredit him, the answer is no. I've studied their records. There are a number of instances in the past when that same pair have picked up men late at night on a drunk and disorderly charge. On more than one occasion the man is said to have assaulted them. In this case they were particularly anxious to round off their patrol with a charge and a conviction."

"Why?"

"Because they'd missed out on an office-breaking job earlier in the evening and had found a reprimand waiting for them when they reported back to the station at midnight."

167

"I see," said the Chancellor with distaste. He knew, as well as anyone, that the best police forces have a sprinkling of unreliable characters. It pained him only to have his attention drawn to it.

"On the other hand," said the Director, "if you're suggesting that the government were embarrassed by Mauger's article, and the attention it drew to the Killey-Dylan case, I should be inclined to agree with you. That's why I should advise the government—if they asked me, and if they ever listened to my advice—to steer as clear as they possibly can of the whole business."

"It's a counsel of perfection," said the Chancellor coldly. "But I'll see that it's passed on. I shall be personally involved, in any event."

"Oh?"

"I am attending the hearing as *amicus curiae*."

"I see," said the Director. He was aware that the Chancellor, by virtue of his office, had to be both politician and lawyer. It had always seemed to him to be an unhappy arrangement.

Lambard was going out to lunch with his son Jonathan. Jonathan had suggested the date. His father had suggested the venue. He trusted the food and the wine list at his own club more than of any restaurant that his son was likely to be able to afford.

As Lambard sat in his office, he wondered rather sadly what Jonathan wanted. Usually it was money. His taxi was at the door and he was on his way out when the telephone rang. He hesitated, realized that his secretary would not have put the call through if it had not been important, and went back.

When, five minutes later, he walked out to the taxi and the driver said, "Where to, sir?" he stared at him, his thoughts obviously far away. Recalling himself with an effort, he gave the name of his club and climbed in. The taxi driver thought he looked like a man who had either heard bad news which he didn't want to believe, or news so good that he hardly dared to believe it.

Over lunch Jonathan kept the conversation so firmly on polo and regimental shop that his father concluded that he must be angling for a very large loan indeed. They were tucked away in the farthest corner of the guest room, and the table next to them was empty. When the coffee had been poured out, Jonathan cleared his throat and said, "There was one thing I wanted to talk about, Dad."

Lambard reached mentally for his check book.

"I was talking to Bill Sexton on Wednesday. He came to one of our guest nights."

Lambard nodded. He knew that his young partner had a number of army friends and was himself a territorial soldier.

"He was rather worried."

"Really?" said Lambard. "He had no cause to be. We're doing rather well this year."

"Not about the firm. About you."

"Oh?"

Jonathan looked embarrassed but determined, like a young man about to propose marriage for the first time. He said, "You mustn't be annoyed with him. He told me because he thought I ought to know."

"About what?"

"About you being offered a knighthood."

"Oh, that. It's not certain yet. Though they don't usually say anything about it unless it's pretty definite."

"That's just what I mean. They could change their minds, couldn't they?"

His father looked at him curiously. A faint suspicion of what was coming crossed his mind. He said, "Certainly. Until the thing's in the *Gazette* it's just a pie in the sky. I believe that, in theory, the Queen can change her mind even after that."

"Mummy would be terribly disappointed if you don't get it now."

"She might be if she knew anything about it."

"She does. I thought I ought to tell her."

"In that case, you did something extremely stupid."

"I realize that now," said Jonathan, with unexpected humility. "Only when Bill told me, I assumed it was a snip. It wasn't until he rang me up last night that I realized that you might . . . that it might not come off."

"I see," said his father. He waved to the waiter, who came across with boxes of cigars on a tray. Lambard offered them to his son, who shook his head impatiently. He selected one himself, cut the end, and lit it. Then he said, "I suppose Bill told you that I was taking on the Killey case."

"Yes. He explained it all to me. That you thought Killey was being framed by the government. It was because people at the Law Society had unearthed some other case like it. Years and years ago. The whole thing sounded pretty thin to me actually."

"Did it?"

"Suppose you're wrong about it. Suppose it was a coincidence. Coincidences do happen. I remember one of the masters at school told me that three different chaps invented logarithms, in three different countries, at the same moment."

His father looked at his son through a haze of cigar smoke. He saw the handsome self-assured petulant face and tried to build it back into the little boy that he had known only a dozen years before. But the child had gone, gone forever.

He said, as gently as he could, "This isn't a mistake, Johnnie. The earlier case was brought by a man called Herman. This one was a man called Stukely. They're the same man. Herman changed his name by deed poll to Stukely some years ago. I heard just before I came out. The Law Society have found the record."

When Mrs. Warburton got to the office, as she was the first to do every morning, she was unable to open the door. Her key went into the lock and turned for a certain distance, then it stuck, and no effort of hers would rotate it far enough to free the catch. Young Willoughby, who arrived shortly afterward, was unable to do much better.

Willoughby said, "If I use much more force, I'll snap the key. There's something in the lock. It's not dirt. It's something hard."

At this point Jonas arrived. He examined the lock and sent Deborah out to fetch the ironmonger from his shop at the other end of Coalporter Street. The ironmonger arrived with a probe and a length of wire and after a few minutes of fiddling extracted the fragment of metal that was jamming the lock and got the door open.

"Stone the crows," he said. "Someone's been having a party, no error."

The outer office was a sea of papers. Filing cabinets had been opened and the contents strewn over the floor. The mess in the other rooms was worse. Every drawer in Jonas' desk had been emptied by the simple process of pulling it out and upending it. The top drawer, which he kept locked, had been smashed.

Books had been swept out of the shelves. Folders of papers had been torn open and the contents added to the pile in the middle of the room.

The ironmonger said, "I'll give the police a ring from my shop. Not much good trying to use that."

The telephone had been pulled off the wall.

The police sergeant who arrived examined the chaos with an experienced eye. He said, "Doesn't look as if they were after money. They'd have gone straight to the safe."

"I don't think they were after money," said Jonas. He sounded unperturbed, almost uninterested. "Actually I think they were after some papers."

"Something important?"

"Important to them. But they didn't find them."

"And how would you know that, sir?"

"Because if I'm right, the things they were looking for are in my own lawyer's strongroom up in Holborn."

The sergeant considered this. He said, "Well, sir, if you know what they were looking for, you must have some idea who it was did the job."

"Oh, I have," said Jonas. "It was Her Majesty's Government."

The sergeant looked at Jonas suspiciously. Then he said, "Mr. *Killey?* Mr. *Jonas* Killey? Aren't you the man they've been making all that fuss about in the papers?"

"I believe there have been a number of reports. I haven't bothered to read them."

"Thought I recognized the name. I'm going to get the inspector in on this."

"Will it be all right if we start clearing up?"

"Can't do much harm. No fingerprints on papers. Better leave your desk for the moment. We might pick up something off that."

By the time the inspector arrived, a measure of order had been restored. The inspector examined the lock and the piece of metal which had been retrieved from it.

"Professional job," he said. "They used a thin key blank and forced up the catch with it. Works all right in an old lock, when there's plenty of play in the gate. Forced it so hard they broke the tip off."

The sergeant agreed with him. He said, "Must have taken quite a time to do all this. I'd better start asking round. See if anyone noticed anything. No curtains on the windows. Someone may have noticed the light on."

When the sergeant had gone, the inspector said, "Did I understand, sir, that you told Sergeant Borrie you had some idea who might have done this?"

"I was pulling the sergeant's leg," said Jonas. "I've really no idea. I expect the man was after cash. He wasn't equipped to open the safe, so he turned the place upside down."

"But what could he have expected to find?"

"He probably did it out of spite," said Jonas impatiently. "As far as I can see, we don't seem to have lost anything. The desk will have to be repaired and the telephone put back. I've spoken to the post office about that. They're sending an engineer right away."

"I shall have to make a report," said the inspector.

"You do that," said Jonas. He sounded unaccountably cheerful.

A possible reason for this was explained when he sent for Willoughby shortly after midday. "I thought I ought to tell you," he said, "only that little bit of fuss this morning put it out of my head. I've heard from the Law Society. They don't intend to take any further action about Mr. Stukely's complaint."

"They don't—for God's sake. What's made them decide? I mean . . . I'm very glad."

"They came to the conclusion that Mr. Stukely was not likely to prove a reliable witness. Did you succeed in reassembling Mrs. Lampier's file? I must do something about her maintenance claim."

Willoughby returned to his own room and converted an

imaginary try by booting the wastepaper basket over the desk. He was a conscientious young man, and the thought that he might have blotted his copybook at the outset of his professional career had been weighing very heavily on him.

"I wonder *when* he knew," he said. "For God's sake. He might have told me before. A professional misconduct charge. 'Thought I ought to tell you.' The office burgled. 'A little bit of a fuss.' I wonder if anything really *would* upset him."

Half an hour later he found an answer to this. Jonas came into his room. His face was white. He said, "I've just had a call from the nursing home at Woking. My mother's had a turn for the worse. I'm going there right away."

Willoughby made some suitable comment. He had never met Mrs. Killey and could not feel very deeply about her. His immediate reaction was that with Jonas out of the way he could take a decent lunch break. He felt that he could use it.

A favorite lunching place, when he had time to get there and back, was the Ring of Bells on Putney Common. A public house which served a decent variety of food, and where he could usually encounter rugby-playing acquaintances. He fell in with two of them at once and was joined by a third. This involved four rounds of drinks. By the time the last of them had been consumed, Willoughby felt that he was ready to eat.

He shared his small table with a man he thought he had met before but could not quite place. It is difficult to sit face to face with someone, one yard from him, without saying something. Willoughby, who was not a reticent young man at any time and was feeling particularly relaxed and happy at that moment, was soon deep in conversation.

Two further rounds of drinks followed. The man opposite was a year or two older than him and had a pleasant nondescript face. The tie he was wearing had crossed silver quills on a dark red background. Willoughby meant to ask him about it, but the conversation had somehow turned onto his own job. Willoughby was not drunk. But he had reached a point where it seemed easy and natural to confide in a chance-met stranger things that he might not have said at all if he had been strictly sober.

Soon he was telling him about the burglary. The young man was most interested and insisted on ordering another drink.

"If your boss has gone down to this nursing home place at Woking," he said, "it's ten to one he won't be coming back at all today. Might as well make the most of it. After all, it isn't every day you have a burglary to celebrate."

"As a matter of fact," said Willoughby, "it wasn't only the burglary. Something else happened this morning."

The young man was a good listener. The story of Mr. Stukely's appearance and disappearance lost nothing in the telling.

At half past two the shutters went up on the bar, and they drifted out into the street. The young man had a car, and obligingly dropped Willoughby at the end of Coalporter Street. Then he sprinted to the nearest telephone booth and dialed a number.

The news editor of the *Banner* said, "What's that?" and "Come again. Say it slowly, and I'll get someone to take it down." And finally, "I suppose it's true."

"Of course it's true," said the young man. "He works in Killey's office. I took him back there just now, to make sure."

"We'll get people checking up on all the different angles," said the news editor. "You got the name of that nursing home in Woking? Good boy."

Parts of the room were dark; parts were bright, where the afternoon sun struck down through the slats of the venetian blind and laid patterns on the floor.

Killey sat beside the bed. His mother was asleep. He could see the deep lines which life had carved on her face, but sleep had flattened the edges and relaxed the tensions. Her mouth was half open, and she was breathing shallowly.

He had not needed the matron's guarded remarks to tell him that she was slipping downhill.

He had sat there quietly for more than an hour before she opened her eyes. It took her a minute or two to collect herself. When she turned her head to look at Jonas, he saw that she was fully conscious and that there was a gleam of animation in her eyes. Her voice had the sharp edge to it which he remembered.

"What are you doing here?" she said. "You ought to be working."

"I thought I'd take the afternoon off," said Jonas. "How are you?"

"Bored. Lift the blind a bit. I don't like this dim light. It's like being in church."

Jonas discovered how the complex of cords on the blind worked and opened the slats, letting in a flood of light.

"That's better," said his mother. "You don't look too fit yourself. I expect you've been overworking. How's it going?"

Jonas knew what she meant by "it." He said, "It's going all right. We're in the Court of Appeal on Monday."

"The Court of Appeal," said the old lady. "That's where your father ended up. It never did him a scrap of good."

"He won."

"I wasn't talking about winning. I was talking about doing him good. It killed him. You don't call that doing good."

Jonas said patiently, "I don't think that's quite true."

"Of course it's true. Mind you, if he'd known he was going to die the next day, he'd still have gone on with it. He was obstinate. As obstinate as you are."

There was a long silence. The brief spark of animation had died down. Jonas wondered if she had dropped off to sleep again. But she apparently had been thinking. She said, "If I asked you to stop it, would you do that for me?"

"I couldn't," said Jonas.

"Why not?"

"It's gone too far. I couldn't stop now. It wouldn't be possible."

"They're only using you."

"Who are?"

"The newspapers. I've read them. They used your father too. I've got boxes full of them at home. They all said how wonderful he was. A little man standing up to a big company and beating it. They didn't really care. A week later they'd forgotten about him. It'll be the same with you. You realize that?"

The old lady's eyes were snapping. There was more vitality in them than Jonas had seen for months.

"I can't help it," said Jonas. "I didn't ask the papers to join in. I don't need their help."

"You'll get it whether you like it or not, my boy. Once they get hold of you, you belong to them."

"What's all this," said the matron. "We mustn't get excited. It's not good for us. I've brought you both a cup of tea. Then we shall have to turn you out, Mr. Killey. We've got to make your mother comfy for the night."

When Jonas got outside, he found two men waiting for him. They fell in beside him as he walked away. One of them said, "We're from the *Evening Banner,* Mr. Killey. Would you care to comment on a report we've had—"

Jonas quickened his pace until he was nearly running.

"—a report we've had that the Law Society were contemplating proceedings against you but have now decided to drop them."

There was a policeman walking along the opposite pavement. Jonas hailed him. He said, "These men are bothering me. Will you tell them to go away."

"What's all this, now?"

"Press. We were just asking this gentleman a few questions."

"If he doesn't want to talk to you, you've no right to pester him."

"Thank you," said Jonas. He walked off quickly in the direction of the station. The men hesitated, then started to follow more slowly.

"Well," said Deborah to the insinuating young man who had followed her home and was now sitting in the front room, chaperoned by her mother. "I must admit, at the time, I did think it was odd."

"Odd, Miss Massingham?"

"Those two men busting into the office like that. Debt collectors, they called themselves. I mean to say. That's not the way to collect debts, is it?"

"Were they abusive?"

"I don't know about abusive."

"Tell him about the typewriter, Deb," said her mother.

"Oh that." Deborah began to giggle. "They said if we didn't pay up they were going to take away the typewriters. Mrs. Warburton—she's a terrible old stick, really—she'd got a new typewriter that week. An electric one. She just threw herself flat down on top of it."

"Like a hen with its last chicken," suggested the young man imaginatively.

"She is a bit like a hen," agreed Deborah.

"Tell him the bit about going to the bank."

"It was Mr. Willoughby sent me. He gave me a check. I had to take it down and cash it. That was when I met Mr. Stukely. Ever so gentlemanly. He walked back to the office with me."

"I don't quite understand about those two banks and the two different accounts. Do you?"

"Search me," said Deborah. "One bank's the same as another as far as I'm concerned. Why don't you ask Mr. Willoughby?"

"I expect we shall be doing that," said the young man.

The attack on the Law Society came just after Christopher had left the office for the day. The reporter was referred to the head of the Publicity and Public Relations Section, who had no idea what to do with him and passed him on to Laurence Fair-brass, who was working late. Laurence listened to his opening remarks and said, "You must realize that you're asking me to comment on something which, if your facts were right—which I don't admit—would be entirely confidential."

"I realize that. It's just that we've been given this story about a complaint being made against Mr. Killey, and the Law Society deciding not to pursue it. We thought we ought to check up on it."

"Why?"

"He's rather in the public eye at the moment."

"That doesn't constitute a reason for asking impertinent questions."

"It does, actually," said the reporter. "But I can quite see you don't have to answer them. I'd better say 'No comment,' I suppose."

"That's right," said Fairbrass. "No comment. And don't twist it into meaning that everything you've suggested is true but the Society won't comment on it, or I'll run you up in front of the Press Council."

The reporter grinned and departed. As soon as he had gone, Fairbrass dialed Tom Buller's home number.

It was Mrs. Buller who answered. "Tom isn't home yet," she said. "And Laurence, there are two men in the garden. They say they're reporters. They wanted to come into the house and wait for Tom, but I wouldn't let them."

"That's right. Keep 'em out. *And don't let Tom talk to them until he's had a word with me.*"

"Goodness! What's it all about? Has someone been murdered?"

"Much more exciting. You don't get more than half a paragraph for murder nowadays. This is headline stuff."

When Mutt met Christopher at the station, he could see that she was worried. She said, "What have you been doing?"

"Nothing that I know of. Why?"

"The papers have been ringing up. And there's a man who wants to interview you."

By now Christopher had a suspicion of what it was all about. "I hope you didn't say anything."

"How could I? I don't know anything."

"That's true."

When they got home, the press were waiting in the porch— a middle-aged man and a young lady. The young lady had a camera. She seemed to want to take Christopher's photograph.

"Would you mind explaining what this is all about?"

"If I've got it right," said the man, "you're the hero of the story. You work at the Law Society, don't you?"

"Yes."

"And it was you who found the court record—whatever it was —the one that proved that someone was trying to frame Killey."

"Good heavens," Christopher said, "I can't talk about that."

As soon as he had said it, he realized that he had made a mistake. The man said smoothly, "Of course, we appreciate that. It'd be a confidential matter. But from what you say, I assume it *was* you who actually unearthed the document."

Fortunately Christopher was saved from further indiscretion by his son. Toby had taken a dislike to the strange man and announced it by starting to scream. The girl said, "Oh, poor darling," put down her camera, and picked him up. This was a false move. Toby was immediately sick all over her.

They had got rid of the press and were having their supper when the telephone rang.

Christopher hesitated before answering it.

"Go on," said Mutt. "It mightn't be them."

It was Tom Buller. He said, "I rang up to find if you'd had any trouble."

"There were some reporters."

"I hope you didn't say anything."

180

"I don't think so."

"If they bother you again, all you have to say is 'No comment.' And if they won't go away, send for the police."

"All right."

In bed that night Mutt said, "It may be all right for people in the public eye, but I don't like it. I'm a private sort of person. I think it's terrifying when people can come into your house and take photographs and ask you questions and write things about you."

Christopher said, "I don't suppose they'll bother us again. They've got bigger fish to fry."

In the days of the semaphore and the horsed courier it may have been possible to nurse a good scoop. Nowadays, no real news can hope to remain exclusive for more than an hour.

The other evening papers had already started covering the *Banner* story in their own Friday night editions. On Saturday morning the national press opened the doors of the furnace.

The story the papers told to millions of breakfast tables on that flaming Saturday morning was, in simple outline, that the government had become embarrassed at Killey's attacks on their fair-haired boy Will Dylan, that a government agency had attempted to discredit Killey, *and that the attempt had misfired.*

The implications of this were clear, the possibilities boundless. Though the legal trumpets were still somewhat muted by the threat of "sub judice," this could not silence the political orchestra. The knowledge that a general election was pending added an extra shrillness to its tone.

"*We* started it," said John Charles to his staff with justifiable pride. "It was *our* story. We're not going to let the other bastards pinch all the gravy. Follow it up, hard."

The leader of the Opposition went down to Smith Square to a meeting of his policy-making body. None of them was under any illusions as to the importance and impact of the news.

"It's the timing that's so critical," said the shadow Home Secretary. "They can't leave the announcement of the dissolution much later than Wednesday week."

"And the High Court hearing starts on Monday?"

"That's right. I understand it's likely to last two days. The court usually gives its decision immediately on a mandamus. That means that we could have a decision by Tuesday afternoon."

The leader considered the matter, sucking on the long-stemmed briar pipe which was his comfort in times of stress. Opinions differed as to his statesmanlike qualities, but he was a noted tactician, a formidable in-fighter in political brawling.

He said, "As I see it, it doesn't really matter which way the court decides. If they quash the application, it will be the Establishment trying to cover up for the government. If they allow the application, there'll be a strong supposition that this man—what's his name?"

"Killey."

"Everyone will believe that Killey is right and Dylan's a crook. I take it that even if Killey wins in this court, he can't possibly mount a criminal prosecution before the autumn."

"I shouldn't think so," said the shadow Attorney General. "He's got to go back to the magistrate first to get his summons. Then he's got to get the committal proceedings going. The defense would be bound to ask for an adjournment. They'd get it, too."

"Good," said the leader. "Then we can forget the law and think about policy. The main thing, as I see it, is not to overplay our hand. What we want is a question in the House on Wednesday. It will have to be framed very carefully. Don't forget that Dylan's popular. He's got a lot of friends. We don't want to appear to aim directly at him. Not yet anyway. What I suggest is a question to the Attorney General. 'In view of the public disquiet, will he direct the Law Society to publish the facts? Were proceedings contemplated against Killey? Were they abandoned? And if so, why?' And I don't think we want to involve the front bench."

"Get Gooley to do it," suggested the shadow Home Secretary. Gooley was a raucous back-bencher, noted for asking tactless questions on any topic at all.

The leader considered the suggestion but vetoed it. He said, "Questions asked by Geoff Gooley aren't always taken seriously. Put Henderson up."

The Commissioner of Metropolitan Police called by appointment on the Home Secretary. The Home Secretary came immediately to the point. He said, "The Killey case—you know what I'm talking about, Commissioner?"

"Yes," said the Commissioner. "I know what you're talking about."

"It comes in front of the High Court on Monday. I don't want the sort of disturbances that occurred at Bow Street to be repeated."

"Do we anticipate them?"

"You've read the reports. Do you think the disturbance at Bow Street was a spontaneous expression of dissent by the friends of the accused on the *Watchman* staff?"

"No, I don't. The men who were removed from the court had nothing to do with the *Watchman*. They were members of an extreme left-wing organization."

"Exactly. And those are the same sort of people who are going to try to whip up a disturbance when this case comes on. I want it stopped."

"The High Court's not like Bow Street. It's a difficult place to seal off. Entrances in the Strand, Carey Street and Bell Yard, and from the courtyard on the west side."

"I don't care how many entrances there are. They've all got

to be checked. No one goes into the building who hasn't got genuine business there. Counsel, solicitors, and their clients."

"I suppose we ought to let the judges in as well," said the Commissioner.

The Home Secretary looked up sharply. He said, "Personally, I don't find the situation amusing."

The Commissioner had seen three home secretaries come and go and was not unduly impressed by them. In his opinion the present holder of that office was the weakest of the three, and like all weak men, was an advocate of strong measures. He said, "It won't be amusing for us, I assure you. We shall have to check a lot of credentials, and people will be kept waiting and will get upset. Also, the general public has a right of access to the public galleries. They won't appreciate being kept out of them. I'm not sure, constitutionally, that we can."

"I'm aware of the difficulties," said the Home Secretary. "I look to you to overcome them."

"We'll do our best," said the Commissioner smoothly.

Back in his office he summoned the appropriate officials and gave instructions. He said, "I don't think we'll have the mounted branch in on this. It's not very effective and tends to annoy people."

One of his subordinates said, "This chap Killey. Will there be any difficulty about getting him into court?"

"Certainly not. He's now so popular they'll probably try to carry him in shoulder high. By the way. Does anyone know where he is at the moment?"

Nobody did know.

"Find out," said the Commissioner. "It might be a good idea to keep an eye on him."

They were not the only people looking for Jonas Killey.

The press, in search of follow-up information, had experienced mixed fortunes with the minor characters. The iron hand of Tom Buller had clamped down on the Law Society, and there was nothing but "No comment" to be had from that source. Lambard had retreated behind the plea of professional privilege and a chained front gate while Jonathan ostentatiously exercised two boxer bitches on the front drive.

Mrs. Warburton, who would have been a primary source of information, escaped trouble by accident. She decided on Friday evening to visit her sister who lived at Bognor Regis, and since it did not occur to her to tell anyone of her plans, she spent a quiet weekend at that resort, returning by an early train on Monday.

Deborah was available. In a sense she was too available. She had only one story to tell, and she told it to everyone. Her mother encouraged her ·and acted as commentator. She had always considered that her daughter had talents which were wasted in a solicitor's office, and she knew that publicity was a key which unlocked many doors.

Young Willoughby was confined to barracks by his father. Mr. Willoughby senior held much the same views about press publicity as Mutt did. He thought that it was a bad thing and that the intrusion of reporters into an Englishman's home was an impertinence, to be met in the same spirit that he and his contemporaries had met the attempted intrusions of Hitler and Goering. He bolted the front and back doors, closed the curtains on all the windows to baffle the photographers, and prepared to sit it out. Had the enemy entered the front garden, he was prepared to counterattack, and he had a stirrup pump, a relic of the last war, ready primed in the hall.

After sitting in semi-darkness for most of that Saturday, Willoughby got fed up, escaped by the kitchen window, and made his way down to the local. Here he was recognized by the press. A number of his rugby-playing acquaintances were on hand as well, and a warm five minutes ended with the reporters being thrown out onto the pavement.

Will Dylan, being a public figure, had secretaries and assistants who were experienced in the routine of keeping the press at a distance. Pauline took the additional precaution of removing the gangplank which led to their houseboat.

But where, in all this, was the principal figure, the man that everyone wanted to talk to?

When his mother was taken to hospital, Jonas had abandoned the empty house and engaged a room in a small private hotel at Crouch End. The pack, making for it in full cry, had sustained a check.

The proprietor of the hotel, a former officer in the Royal Navy, had himself suffered from the attentions of the press over an unfortunate incident involving the ramming of a light cruiser by a destroyer at Scapa Flow. He had been waiting for a long time to tell the press what he thought about them, and he seized the opportunity with both hands.

The reporters retired to lick their wounds, keep observation on the hotel, and await Jonas' return.

They waited in vain, for in fact Jonas had left the hotel on the Friday to attend the conference with counsel and had not returned.

He was not hiding, nor was he running away. He knew that all the necessary preparations had been made for the High Court hearing on Monday and that there was nothing more that he personally could do either before it or—since the proceedings would be on affidavit—at it. It seemed to him to be a good opportunity to carry out a plan which had been forming in his mind for some days.

He caught an evening train from Waterloo to Salisbury, and a bus at Salisbury which ran out in the dusk of yet another long sunlit day, past Old Sarum and Boscombe Down and out onto the plain. He was making for a small hotel which he had been told of between Netheravon and Upavon which catered mainly for fishermen. He was not interested in fishing but was a dedicated walker, and it had occurred to him that the open spaces of Salisbury Plain would give him the sort of exercise he was looking for.

He also needed to think, and walking and thinking were things which he had found went well together.

The hotel—it was little more than an inn really—had six bedrooms, and he was lucky enough to find one of them empty. At dinner he met the other residents—two elderly fishermen, two elderly fishermen's wives, and a clergyman—and after dinner they all sat together in the lounge, which was also the saloon bar, and a number of the local inhabitants drifted in for their evening drinks and stayed to talk.

Everyone seemed concerned and excited about something in the newspapers, and in the end by piecing scraps of comment together Jonas gathered what it was. The County Council had published plans for a feeder road to join the M.5. at Amesbury, which might bring it through the village. No one approved of this. At half past ten Jonas went up to his attic bedroom and slept.

Next morning after breakfast, with some sandwiches in his pocket, he set out to walk. The sun was still riding in glory over a parched land, but the heat was a lot less oppressive than it had been in London streets. When he reached the top of Rushall Down, a tiny breeze was wandering across the empty miles of green and brown upland, and he could hear guns booming away on the artillery ranges to the south.

He ate his sandwiches with his back propped up against a concrete structure, which was something the army had put up and forgotten about; and in the early afternoon he came down off the escarpment into the village of Sambourne. Its full name, as he discovered from a signpost, was Sambourne-in-the-Vale. It had a single long village street which ran out eventually to the main road, where there was a bus shelter. Also there was a church, with an overgrown churchyard, one large house, a couple of dozen smaller ones, a pub called the Eagle and Child, and a general store which was also a post office.

Jonas found the church open and wandered in. It was a hotchpotch of styles and of no great architectural merit. He gathered from the names on a number of slabs and tablets that the big house had belonged for many generations to a family called Lamplough.

When he came back into the empty, dozing main street, his eye was attracted by a handwritten notice in the window of the general store. He walked across to read it, and after he had finished reading, he stood there so long staring into the window that the owner came to the conclusion that the strange thin man in a well-worn but citified flannel suit must be contemplating a smash-and-grab raid.

There was an element of truth in this. An idea which had come into Jonas' head on the evening when he had visited Edgar Dyson at his little house in the suburbs of Sheffield, and which had taken firmer root when he realized that his mother was dying, appeared now in concrete form.

He went into the store. One long wall was covered with shelves which held a great variety of goods arranged in no particular order. A counter ran along the opposite side holding other goods, some in cardboard display stands, others heaped at random. The far corner was shut off by a grille, behind which an old lady sat conducting the business of the postmaster general.

When she discovered that Jonas had no aggressive intentions, she fell into conversation with him. It was half an hour before he emerged and started the long tramp home.

Interest in the lounge that night was divided between a speech made by one of the county councilors, who was opposed to the new road, and a two-and-a-half-pound trout caught by one of the elderly fishermen. They also heard a good deal about a much larger trout which the other elderly fisherman had failed to land.

On Sunday morning Jonas went back to Sambourne by bus. He arrived in time for the morning service, at the conclusion of which he buttonholed the vicar and had a long talk, which ended with him being invited to lunch at the rectory, a building he had not spotted before, since it was hidden, in the manner of country rectories, behind a rampart of laurels.

In the late afternoon he walked back across Black Heath and Thornham Down. The gunners were observing the sabbath, and it was quiet enough to hear the larks which before the army came had given Larkhill its name.

The inn too was quiet that evening. The fishermen had finished their holiday and gone home. The landlord asked Jonas if he wanted to keep his room. Jonas, who had reached certain tentative conclusions that day, said that he would like to keep the room for at least a week. He said, "I might have to run up to London a couple of times, but I'd aim to be back here each night if possible."

"Must be quite a change here after London," said the landlord. Jonas agreed that this was so.

After dinner he telephoned the nursing home at Woking and had a reassuring bulletin. The landlord offered to bring his wireless set into the lounge, but Jonas refused.

"Don't blame you," said the landlord. "There's never much news on a Sunday."

"It's a strong court," said Wilfred Cairns.

Flanking the Lord Chief Justice on one side was Mr. Justice Megan, thin and scholarly, with the fleshless face of a hermit, noted for his wit, as dry as the sherry he drank. On the other side was the robust figure of Mr. Justice Lamb, "Larry" to the four Inns of Court. He had started the war as a guardsman and had finished as a general staff officer and was the soundest academic lawyer of the three.

"I appear for the appellant, Jonas Killey," said Cairns. "My learned friend Mr. Pallant appears for the respondent magistrate, Mr. Cedric Lyon, and the learned Attorney General appears as *amicus curiae*. My client is seeking an order of this court, in the form of a writ of mandamus, directing the respondent magistrate to rehear the application which he made before him on June twenty-eighth last."

The reasons that had led Lambard to choose Wilfred Cairns were apparent in his manner, in his voice, in the way he addressed the court, and in the way the court listened to him. He possessed the one priceless gift which had destined him for the bench from the moment he first donned a barrister's white wig —the gift of *gravitas*. His courtesy to his opponents was complete, his purpose to defeat them was inflexible.

"During the course of these proceedings," he said, "I shall be forced to criticize both the law as propounded by the learned magistrate and his conduct of the case. I will deal with these matters separately, starting with a consideration of the law. In my submission this was correctly stated by the learned magistrate, but unfortunately was not applied by him. He stated at one point that all the appellant had to do was to make out a prima facie case. Strict proof of his allegations would only be necessary when the matter came before the appropriate tribunal. This must be right. If it were not right, the same matter would, in effect, have to be tried twice over."

"In which case," said Mr. Justice Megan, "might not the appellant put forward a plea of autrefois convict or autrefois acquit on the second occasion?"

"I had not thought of taking the argument quite so far," said Cairns with a slight smile, "but it might, I suppose, be so."

"I think the court must grant you that much," said the Lord Chief Justice. "But the matter still turns on what ought reasonably to be regarded as prima facie proof that an offense has been committed."

"I am not proposing to evade that issue. The point I am seeking to make is that strict proof was a matter properly reserved for the hearing of the case. And that this consideration applied equally to the evidence which the applicant put forward *and to the documents which he produced.* I may perhaps remind you that there were three main documents. The first was a set of accounts made out by Dylan, the man against whom he sought the summons. Dylan was secretary and treasurer of what I will call the smaller union. The second was the amalgamation agreement between the smaller union and the larger union. The third was the annual return of the larger union. The first two of these were, in a sense, private documents, documents of which an outsider would be unlikely to possess the originals. What the appellant *did* manage to produce was a copy of the first and a made-up draft of the second, both of which had come into his hands in the course of his previous employment in a solicitors' office in Sheffield. Whether he should have removed them from that office in the first place is, of course, a different matter, but one which does not, in my view, affect their validity."

"Even if it were shown that they were stolen," said Mr. Justice Lamb.

"Even if they were stolen. I shall be referring later to the case of Carfax against Carfax, in which a foreign birth certificate was admitted as evidence even though it had been stolen, by force, from the defendant."

"But a birth certificate, Mr. Cairns," said the Lord Chief Justice, "is a document of public record which proves itself, from whatever source it is produced."

"With respect, my lord, that would only be so if it was a British birth certificate."

The Lord Chief Justice looked out of the corner of his eye at Mr. Justice Lamb, who nodded imperceptibly.

The Lord Chief Justice said, "Of course. I had forgotten that it was a foreign certificate. Proceed, Mr. Cairns."

The main force of police concentrated on the front of the building. Interlocked steel barriers had been set up along the edge of the pavement on the court side of the road, and behind these barriers was ranged a single and continuous line of policemen. What was left of the pavement was free for people who wished to pass, but no one was allowed to loiter. Demonstrators were confined to the pavement on the far side of the road. Reserve contingents of police were stationed at the different entrances to the building, including the entrance to the public galleries, a point which caused a good deal of comment later. A mobile patrol was considered sufficient for Bell Yard, which is separated from the building by a car park flanked by high railings and a padlocked gate. The west side was similarly protected. In both cases entry to the car parks was confined to court officials with regulation passes.

The rear of the court backs on Carey Street. Here the police tenders were parked nose to tail. A command post in a radio car at the junction of Bell Yard and Carey Street kept in touch with the main force in front. There were small groups of policemen at the judges' entrance and the lawyers' entrance, which were the only two left open at the rear, but it was not thought necessary to form a continuous line.

"We're using over a hundred policemen as it is," said Chief Superintendent Hallet, who was in charge of the operation. "If trouble does start round the back, we can bring reinforcements up through one of the car parks quickly enough."

The B.B.C. commentator, whose van was tucked away in Serle Street, said, "There seem to be more policemen about than members of the public. The only difficulty which is being caused is to people who have legitimate business in the courts and are being held up and questioned. A queue is forming at the entrance reserved for barristers and solicitors, and since all the courts start business promptly at ten-thirty, this has caused a lot of annoyance. Our reporter spoke to one of the people involved."

An angry young man appeared on the screen and said, "The whole thing's nonsensical. No one seems to know what it's in aid of. If it's just the Killey case, why don't they block off that court. There's no reason to turn the whole bloody place into a fortress."

"Thank you very much," said the commentator. "I asked the police officer in charge for his views, but he refused to comment."

"I think," said the Lord Chief Justice, glancing at the clock, which showed a few minutes after twelve, "that we have heard all the submissions which are likely to be of assistance to us in considering the admissibility and weight of the different documents. I understood you to say, Mr. Cairns, that you were going to deal next with the learned magistrate's conduct of the case."

"That is so, my lord. And I have here to put in an affidavit by a reporter on the staff of the *Watchman* to which is exhibited a verbatim transcript of the proceedings."

Mr. Pallant was already on his feet. "I must object."

"Yes, Mr. Pallant?"

"This document, which I have seen, is not an official transcript in the sense in which the expression is understood in these courts. It is extracts, originally in shorthand, from the notebook of a newspaper reporter who happened to be in court, which have been transcribed into longhand. In my view such a document would have been totally inadmissible as evidence and cannot be brought before the court by the device of exhibiting it as an affidavit."

"With respect," said Cairns, "it is a contemporaneous record kept by a person whose duty it was to keep such a record. He did not *happen* to be in court. He was there because it was his duty to be there."

"A duty for which, I imagine, he was paid a large sum," said Mr. Justice Megan.

"I am not sure how much he was paid, my lord. But he certainly did not keep this record for his own edification or amusement."

"Cases in the past bearing on this point," said Pallant, "have been confined to records kept by deceased functionaries—policemen, warders, probation officers, and other persons of this sort—in the course of their official duty. I have found no instance of a written record made by a private person who is still alive being admitted."

"But is a reporter a private person?" said Mr. Justice Lamb.

"Might I refer you," said Cairns smoothly, "to the case of Penruddock against the Rochester Bridge Wardens . . ."

At half past twelve a middle-aged man wearing a morning

coat, striped trousers, a waistcoat made from a Union Jack, and a top hat which had a notice, "Liberty of All Citizens," pasted to the front, advanced along the barricaded pavement in front of the court to an accompaniment of cheers from the considerable crowd now collected on the pavement opposite. As he came level with the entrance to the public gallery, he swung suddenly to his left and darted through. The maneuver took the group of policemen so much by surprise that it almost succeeded. One of them grabbed his flying coattails and pulled him back. The man, wriggling like a gaffed fish, slipped out of his coat but was grabbed by a second policeman around the waist.

The crowd on the opposite pavement took this badly. There were shouts of "Leave him alone," "Pick on someone your own age," and "Shame." A large and overripe tomato sailed across the road and hit a policeman in the face. The crowd started to advance across the road.

"Reserves from Bell Yard, clear the road," said Hallet.

A squad of policemen who had been waiting for the word emerged from the mouth of Bell Yard and forced their way down the street using their combined weight, hustling and treading on toes until the road was clear and the traffic piled up in the Strand and Fleet Street could move on again.

The middle-aged man, his shirttails flapping but his top hat still wedged defiantly on his head, was carried by four policemen to a tender. Onlookers cheered. Cameras flashed.

"No trouble really," said Hallet into the radiotelephone link with Central. "One crackpot who tried to get into the building in fancy dress. He put up some sort of fight, and we're holding him for the moment, but I don't think we'll be making a charge. The crowd's a lot thinner now than it was this morning. We ought to be able to send some of our men home this afternoon."

"In the expectation—or perhaps I should say the hope—that your lordships *would* admit Mr. Mauger's record," said Cairns,

196

"I have had sufficient copies prepared for the court, and I will ask the usher to hand them up. My learned friend has a copy already."

Pallant smiled briefly. He had indeed read Patrick Mauger's record, had recognized its damaging potentialities, and had fought hard, giving back precedent for precedent, to prevent its production. The Attorney General had attempted to support him, but had, in Pallant's view, been more of a hindrance than a help by trying to pull rank and bully the Lord Chief Justice. It was common knowledge that the Lord Chief Justice loathed him.

He glanced at the clock on the wall. It showed five minutes to three. It looked as though a second day was going to be necessary. This was a nuisance, as it would mean surrendering the brief in a company matter which was a great deal more to his taste than quasi-political wrangling.

"I do not propose," said Cairns, "to take you line by line through this bulky exhibit, but would refer you only to one or two extracts which I have marked. At page seven, halfway down the page, you will see the following:

" 'KILLEY: With regard to the instrument of amalgamation, I am in this position that I am only able to produce a made-up draft.

" 'MAGISTRATE: A what, Mr. Killey?

" 'KILLEY: A made-up draft.

" 'MAGISTRATE: I don't understand. Do you mean it is some document you have made up yourself? (Laughter)

" 'KILLEY: As you are perfectly well aware, a made-up draft is a copy of the final document into which such details as the date and the names of the signatories have been inserted.

" 'MAGISTRATE: You mustn't tell me what I'm aware of and what I'm not aware of. It's for you to make your application in a proper way.

" 'KILLEY: I am trying to do so. In the face of considerable obstruction.'

"I have read you that extract, which is typical of many, because it seems to me to demonstrate what went wrong. I need not remind you that the magistrate was a lawyer and must have known perfectly well what a made-up draft signified. On the other hand, I would concede that the applicant was not an easy man to deal with. There were occasions when he demonstrated less than a proper respect for the court. But in my view this ought not to have prevented the learned magistrate from coming to an unbiased decision on the merits of the application. I am sure that your lordships have, on occasions, been provoked by the conduct of persons appearing before you, but this has not prevented you from arriving at a dispassionate assessment."

This produced the smile that Cairns had anticipated. There had been an occasion, not long before, in which an infuriated female litigant, who was conducting her own case, had thrown a lawbook at the Lord Chief Justice. It had been widely reported.

"Again, at page eleven, final paragraph, we find:

" 'KILLEY: The point I am trying to make is entirely supported by the authority of the case of Foss against Harbottle.

" 'MAGISTRATE: Who against who?

" 'KILLEY: If we had that window shut, you might be able to hear me better.

" 'MAGISTRATE: If the window is shut, the court becomes quite intolerably hot.

" 'KILLEY: It's not much use my going on, if you're not going to listen to what I have to say.

" 'MAGISTRATE: Whether you go on or not, Mr. Killey, is entirely a matter for you. I happen to regard the comfort of people in my court as more important than the convenience of advocates. You will have to speak more clearly.'

"You will find, however, that when the learned magistrate came to announce his decision—it is at page twenty-two—he *did* have the window closed. No doubt he wished everyone to hear what he had to say. Now I have already made my submissions on the substance of that judgment. I think it was wrong in law. But whatever the court's view may be on that, there can, in my submission, be no doubt at all that the final comment which the learned magistrate saw fit to make was so uncalled for that it must color and cast doubt on all that had gone before."

The attack came in at three o'clock precisely. It was preceded by a diversionary maneuver. Half a dozen men started to climb rather slowly over the railings of the car park behind the Queen Elizabeth Building at the west end of the court. Chief Superintendent Hallet had been as good as his word and had thinned out the cordon in Carey Street. Most of the men who were left ran to intercept the climbers.

At this moment an assault group burst from the passageway which leads from New Square. The front rank were carrying mattresses. They jumped up onto the sand bin which stands conveniently in an angle of the railings next to one of the padlocked gates, threw the mattresses over the iron spikes of the railing, and held them in place while the men behind swarmed over and dropped onto the steps behind. These led directly to an unlocked back door of the court building.

The two policemen still left at that point were jostled to one side. The ones who had been drawn away, realizing almost too late that they had been fooled, swung around and raced back. It was one of them who flung himself at a climbing figure and got hold of his ankles, at the same moment that one of his friends already safely across, grabbed his arms to pull him over.

If the mattress had stayed in place, it might not have mattered, but it slipped to one side and the steel spike which it had covered was driven into the body of the man straddled across it.

"I imagine, Mr. Pallant," said the Lord Chief Justice, "that you will have something to say about the extracts which have been read to us."

"I have a number of observations to make," said Pallant. And this was all that he did say, since at this moment the van of the intruders reached the court. The door was flung open with a crash. Pallant turned to see what was happening. The two ushers rose in scandalized protest to their feet. Half a dozen men were in the room already, shouting and waving banners, with reinforcements crowding in behind them. High above the growing tumult sounded the clarion voice of Ben Thomas. "Justice. We want justice."

The next few minutes might have been less confused if the court had not already been crowded. In spite of the precautions of the police a great many people seemed to have made their way, on one pretext or another, into the building, and most of them were in the court. One of the intruders jostled a burly solicitor's clerk, who hit back. Battle became general. The weapons used were fists and feet, the missiles lawbooks, inkpots, and anything else to hand.

The junior bar was engulfed in the fighting. The two leaders and the Attorney General scuttled toward the bench. Only the three judges preserved their dignity. Taking their time from the Lord Chief Justice, they rose to their feet, bowed punctiliously, first to the bar, and then to the body of the court, and left the scene of conflict without haste.

Outside in the corridor came the pounding of feet as the first police reinforcements started to arrive.

Superintendent Hallet reported to Central. "It's under control now. We've arrested about twenty of the ringleaders. We know most of them. Hard-line troublemakers."

Central said something. Hallet said, "It was an accident. They've taken him to the Middlesex. He was still alive when they got him there. But they don't hold out much hope. The spike went through the bottom of the ribs and the top of the abdomen. The real damage was done when they pulled him off."

The man at the other end said, "Hold on, Superintendent. The Commissioner has something he wants to say to you."

The Commissioner of Police for the metropolis said in a voice which crackled, "You realize, I hope, the seriousness of the situation. No statement or comment of any sort is to be made by you, or any of your men. The matter will be handled by me personally, from this moment. You understand?"

Superintendent Hallet said unhappily that he understood.

The press understood too. And the people were beginning to understand.

The heart of the great British public is cold and hard to stir. It has a built-in inertia factor, a massive skepticism. It has been braced too often to face nonexistent crises; titillated by hints of unborn scandals which never come to birth; stirred by banner headlines which bear, on closer examination, as little relationship to the story underneath as the shouts of the barker to the exhibits in the tent.

But now, at the last moment, a perception that something of real significance had happened began to dawn. The fruits of that broiling July were being gathered at high speed. The harvest was coming home.

The front-page headline of the *Watchman*, in a size of type which had not been used since 1939, consisted of one word: "Impaled." The cartoonist, pursuing the same theme, showed the figure of justice transfixed on an iron railing with frock-coated figures on one side, representing the government, pulling at its legs, and the bewigged representatives of the law hanging on to its arms on the other side.

The Opposition papers screamed down like dive bombers on an undefended convoy.

"We are entitled to ask . . ." said the *Daily Mentor,* using one of its favorite openings. It then proceeded to ask itself a number of unanswerable questions. Had a government agency in fact had a hand in an attempt to discredit Jonas Killey? Had the Law Society unmasked the plot and defeated it? Was there a connection between yesterday's riot in the High Court and a recent attack on the police in a case at Bow Street? And finally, why had the Attorney General seen fit to interest himself in what appeared to be a private application by a citizen for a writ of mandamus? Ought not the Prime Minister to make a statement to set at rest the very disquieting stories which had now received considerable currency? The foreign press was beginning to comment, and national prestige was at stake.

It was left for the *Times* to sum matters up. Until this point it had been notably reticent, dealing with the news in short paragraphs and refraining from comment. Now it reverted suddenly to its traditional role. Olympus awoke. The Thunderer spoke.

"What we are faced with," it said, "is nothing less than the old struggle, which historians would persuade us was finally won in this country more than two hundred years ago with the Act of Settlement: the struggle between the executive and the judiciary. Yet, in spite of all the fair words which have been spoken, it remains a hard, inescapable fact that those who govern are irked by the fetters of the law. Law is an excellent thing for the governed, no doubt. It teaches them their duties and keeps them in their place. But it must not be allowed to control or constrict the governors. They have a task and a duty which must sometimes override the law. *Salus populi suprema lex.* The safety of the state is above the law. It is an attractive notion. It is also the first step towards despotism. For there is a second, an older and a wiser Latin tag. *Fiat justitia ruat coelum.* Let justice be done though the sky fall. And if we may allow for the fall of the sky, surely we can contemplate with comparative equanimity the fall of a government which has seen fit to disregard the law. A government which has dirtied its hands . . ."

The leader of the Opposition said to a full meeting of the shadow Cabinet, "They won't be able to put off the announcement of the dissolution for more than a few days. Keep up the pressure. We have been laying off Dylan. Now we must go for him."

This produced a murmur of approval.

"Have we got to be a bit careful of contempt of court?" said the shadow Home Secretary.

"Only if you comment on the actual mandamus proceedings," said the shadow Lord Chancellor. "Even then you'd probably get away with it on the grounds of overriding public interest."

"What about Killey? Wouldn't it be a good idea to give him a bit of a build-up. That couldn't do any harm."

"I understand that he's gone underground," said the leader. "But I imagine the press will unearth him."

The Prime Minister walked down that afternoon from the House to Smith Square. He enjoyed walking in London when the weather was fine. It gave him a rare opportunity to stretch his legs. The only person who found this habit a trial was his private detective.

At the headquarters of the party the two men who worked behind the scenes but were of decisive influence in the party machine were waiting for him. The chairman, a man who never minced his words, said, "Two months ago, Prime Minister, I told you that Dylan was worth thirty or forty seats to us. If things are allowed to go on as they are, he may still be worth that number of seats—to the Opposition."

"It couldn't have happened at a worse moment," said the deputy chairman.

"I agree," said the Prime Minister. "When do we expect the verdict?"

"The court reserved judgment. They don't usually do it, but it was an unusual case. They promised to announce it early next week."

The Prime Minister considered the matter. He said, "That brings us to the twenty-ninth or thirtieth. If our friends over the way had stage-managed it, they could hardly have arranged it better. Is this chap Killey going to get his mandamus?"

"The buzz is that it's two to one," said the deputy chairman. "Megan's for him, because he thinks the magistrate behaved like a buffoon. He ought to be a good judge of that. He's always making bad jokes in court."

"What about Lamb?"

"He thinks the magistrate was stupid, but was right in law. The Lord Chief has been wobbling, but may come down on Killey's side because he can't stand the Attorney General. I don't suppose anyone really knows, but that's supposed to be the form."

"It's unimportant," said the Prime Minister. "Whichever way they decide, it's going to hurt us."

The chairman said, "Yes," and looked at him speculatively.

"If you think the matter through," said the Prime Minister, "you'll find the real trouble is that the public has heard Killey's side of the story—heard it in a dozen different versions. But there's been no opportunity of giving Dylan's. If it comes to court, I've no doubt of his getting an honorable acquittal. I think the charge is stale and spiteful nonsense without a particle of real evidence to back it up. But an acquittal will come too late to be of any use. I mean, of course, too late to be of use to the party. It will be a sort of satisfaction for Dylan, although it's bound to leave a smear. If we're going to rehabilitate him, it's got to be done now."

"A personal statement in the House?"

"I can see no alternative."

The three men considered it. They all knew that a personal statement could be very effective. It could also be completely disastrous. They knew too that by the traditions of the House there would be no debate about it. Where a member's honor was impugned he had the right to make his defense uninterrupted and unquestioned. But because it was no part of the ordinary proceedings of the House, it had to be entirely candid and convincing.

The chairman said, "I think there's one thing we ought to know, Prime Minister. This story about one of the hush-hush departments trying to discredit Killey. Is there any truth in it?"

"If it was done," said the Prime Minister coldly, "I neither knew about it nor consented to it. I am having the matter investigated. If the people concerned took steps on their own authority, they will have to take the consequences. I should like everyone to be quite clear about that."

There was a moment of not very comfortable silence. The deputy chairman broke it by saying, "If Dylan makes a statement, it will at least bring him back into the picture. The odd thing about all this is that the press has been having a field day, but the two people it's supposed to be all about have been remarkably reticent. Dylan hasn't said anything and Killey seems to have disappeared."

"He'll emerge at the appropriate moment," said the chairman sourly, "with a bloody great halo round his stupid head."

Simon Benz-Fisher was whistling gently to himself as he fed a pile of dockets into the huge stove in the basement of Lynedoch House. The existence of this old-fashioned solid fuel system of central heating had been, to him, one of the attractions of the building.

Terence appeared at the entrance of the stokehole with an armful of files. "This is the last of them," he said. "I hope you know what you're doing."

Benz-Fisher looked at the name on the file, chuckled, and said, "I think we might have one or two out of this one." He unclipped the file, riffled through the contents, and finally extracted half a dozen of the letters.

"We've got some photographs belonging to that one," said Terence. "They're in the folder."

"Artistic?"

"Oh, very."

"Then we might keep a couple of them." He added them to the contents of an already bulging brief case.

"What's it all in aid of?" said Terence. "A bit of the old black?"

"My dear Terence—yes, you can put all the rest in. I don't think we've any further use for them—you have known me for five years. Do you really suppose that I am a common or garden blackmailer."

"Honest to God," said Terence, "I don't know what you are, and that's the truth."

Benz-Fisher smiled complacently. "I am all things to all men. I am X, the unknown factor in the equation. I am the Gordian knot, which no human ingenuity can untie. I am a master illusionist."

He looked down into the red heart of the furnace which was sluggishly digesting its diet of paper and cardboard. He took the iron poker and plunged it into the glowing mass, which flared up into little tongues of yellow flame.

"Tomorrow all this, the fruits of so many years' work, will be a handful of gray ashes."

"They won't half be narked when they find out what you've done."

"Let them be narked. Did you ever see that well-known conjuring trick, Terence, when a man makes a girl disappear?"

"I've seen it done once. They said it was done with mirrors."

"I can do an even better trick. And I need no mirrors to perform it. I can wave a wand and make *myself* disappear."

"Sounds a useful trick. You couldn't teach me, I suppose."

"No, Terence. I fear it is beyond you. It requires prudence, patience, and foresight. Gifts which your fairy godmother gives you at birth, or not at all. Allied to this, you need the mind of a chess master. A mind that can construe the tactics of an opponent six months ahead and construct a plan to deal with each possible permutation and combination."

Off again, thought Terence. Right up in the stratosphere.

On the last word Benz-Fisher slammed shut the door of the furnace, perched his bowler hat on his head, picked up his brief case, gave a cheerful wave of his rolled umbrella, and vanished through the doorway.

It *was* a bit like a conjuring trick, thought Terence.

There were a number of reasons why the various parties who were searching for Jonas Killey should have failed to locate him.

One reason was his handwriting. This was so vile that the hotel at which he was staying had registered him as Jacob Kellow and addressed him as Mr. Kellow throughout his stay. The second reason was that he had forgotten, in the excitement of the past month, to get his hair cut. It was now not only much longer than usual, but, feeling self-conscious about the bruise down the side of his face, he had allowed it to descend in embryo sideburns. A more important reason was that the press had been unable to locate a useful photograph. Jonas was not a man who sought publicity, and the best that the researchers had been able to turn up was a school group, taken in his last year at Grantham Grammar School nearly twenty-five years before, and a rather blurred snapshot of a group of solicitors who had attended a seminar on international law in Amsterdam.

But the real reason why nobody spotted Jonas was that he wasn't hiding. He wasn't hiding, because it hadn't occurred to him that anyone was looking for him. If he had behaved in a fugitivelike manner, it is possible he would have been noticed. But he was not a fugitive. He was taking an unscheduled, but extremely enjoyable holiday. The only newspapers he saw were the *Salisbury and Winchester Journal* and the *Andover Herald*, and the headlines in these were devoted to such topics of local interest as an outbreak of arson at Bulford, the new bypass, and suspected foot and mouth disease at Pewsey.

From time to time Jonas thought guiltily of his practice, but he comforted himself with the reflection that it would do young Willoughby a power of good to have a few days at the helm. There was nothing like responsibility for settling a young man down. His only real worry was his mother. He telephoned the nursing home every morning and every evening, and the reports which he received, though tactfully delivered, left him in no doubt as to the truth. Her life was slipping away.

On the Thursday he caught a bus into Salisbury and called on a firm of solicitors in Castle Street. He had telephoned them on the previous afternoon, and the senior partner, Mr. Abigail, saw him at once.

Being a solicitor himself, Jonas appreciated that nine tenths of the instructions which clients give solicitors are superfluous. He confined himself to mentioning the names, addresses, and sums of money which mattered. It took exactly five minutes.

As he rose to go, Mr. Abigail said, "You've been having a short holiday, Mr. Killey?"

"A few days."

"The press not bothering you?"

"No. Why should they?"

After a moment of silence Mr. Abigail said, "Have you seen the papers in the last few days?"

"Only the local ones."

"I suggest you buy the *Times* and the *Telegraph*. Oh, and the *Watchman* too. If you'd like to see Tuesday's and Wednesday's, I can get them for you."

"Please don't bother," said Jonas. "If there's anything interesting in them I can see them when I get back to London."

After he had left, Mr. Abigail took that morning's copy of the *Watchman* out of his brief case and reread the paragraph on page one:

"It was noted that Mr. Killey was not in court either on the Monday when the riot occurred or on the following day when their lordships reserved judgment. Speculation is beginning to grow as to his whereabouts. A spokesman for the police said, 'We have no instructions to investigate Mr. Killey's movements, nor is there any reason why we should have such instructions. Mr. Killey is free to go wherever he wishes.' The central figure in one of the most extraordinary dramas of recent times would seem to have vanished. Enquiries at his Wimbledon office revealed that they had had no word from him since Friday. *Where is Mr. Killey?*"

Mr. Abigail reflected that had professional propriety not forbidden it, the *Watchman* would have paid him handsomely for the answer to that question.

When Jonas got back to his hotel, the message which he had been expecting from the nursing home was waiting for him. He gave the necessary instructions and said that he would be returning on the following day. The matron said, "Very peaceful. No pain at all. She simply went to sleep and didn't wake up." Jonas cut her short by ringing off. He was equally brusque when the proprietor offered his condolences. He said, "I'm going for a walk. I shall be back for supper. Could you have my bill ready."

210

"In this country," said the Prime Minister, "we seem to have overlooked the value of the courts of law as a setting for demonstrations. It wasn't only propaganda trials in the Russian manner that I was thinking of. It is the French, it seems to me, who have perfected the art of the scene in court. I was reading, only yesterday, a new account of the Dreyfus case . . ."

Will Dylan, sitting uneasily in the tall leather-covered armchair stamped with the insignia of the House of Commons, wondered how the Prime Minister had time to read anything except official papers. There was a heap of these on his desk at that moment. He wondered also how long the Prime Minister was going to take to reach what was evidently on his mind. Although he had not been long in Parliament, he was well aware of the speed with which reputations rose and fell, the way in which people were reassessed almost daily, as on a stock exchange, so that a member could be a blue chip one day and a bad buy on the next. He had a shrewd idea of what was coming, but it was no use trying to hurry the old man.

To help things along, he said, "You mean that business in the High Court."

"And that scene at Bow Street. The same men were involved in both."

"I don't see the connection."

"The connection is that they were both aimed at you. The first indirectly, the second directly. They were both designed to draw public attention to the allegations which a solicitor called Killey has been making about you."

When he came to the point, thought Dylan, he came straight there, no fooling.

He said, "You could be right, Prime Minister. I hadn't quite viewed it in that way. What do you want me to do about it?"

"There's only one thing a member of this house can do when his personal reputation is attacked. He has to stand up and defend it. It's a useful privilege. If vague stories are being whispered, vague allegations being made, he can bring them out into the open. Fresh air kills germs. If plain lies are being told, he can nail them. I think the best time will be this evening. I'll have a word with the Opposition, and they'll clear the floor for you at about seven o'clock. That means we shall get full coverage in the morning papers. They're more responsible about that sort of thing than the evening papers."

Will was silent for so long that the Prime Minister raised his head sharply and said, "Well?"

Will said, "Ever since I came down here, Prime Minister, I've been realizing how important words are. It doesn't matter what you do. It doesn't matter if you do nowt, as long as you make the right noises."

"Not entirely true," said the Prime Minister. He was conscious of the strength of the man opposite, a strength of character and bone, showing in the face. He noticed too that, now that he was speaking from the heart rather than the head, Dylan was reverting to a fashion of speech which, consciously or unconsciously, he had modified during his stay in the south. "Some truth in it. Go on."

"This thing you're talking about. It's been on t'boil for a long

212

time. Simmering, you might say, to start with. Now it's come to boil. T'other chap's done all the talking. I've said nowt. I'm not starting now."

"So far as you're concerned, that's a point of view I can understand. In the ordinary way, no one's called on to defend themselves from malicious rumors. But this isn't an ordinary situation. It's got blown up out of all proportion. And it's hurting the party."

"I'm not that important," said Will.

"My party managers tell me a different story."

"Even if it happened to be true, and I'll be blunt with you, it wouldn't keep me awake nights. I'm not a party man. Truth to tell, there doesn't seem to be a lot of difference between parties, except that one's in and t'other's out."

The Prime Minister said, with an edge of exasperation showing for the first time in his voice, "I can't force you to take my advice. But you realize what it'll mean to you if you don't."

Will said with a grin, "If you're taking back your offer of the Ministry of Labor, that's understood."

"I didn't mean that only. I meant to you personally. The sniping will go on. And if Killey gets his order, it'll get a lot worse. I don't doubt that when it finally comes to court, you'll win, but by then it'll be too late. The thing's got to be stopped now, once and for all. If the good of the party doesn't weigh with you, you might at least consider the feelings of your friends, and your family."

As soon as the Prime Minister had said this, he realized that he had made a mistake.

Will said, his face dark with anger, "We've had a basinful already. And I don't only mean anonymous letters. They're as good as newspapers to light fire with. But we've had phone calls at home. And things said to my boy at school. And messages chalked up by some crackpot on the houseboat I'm living in. But I got one letter this morning that wasn't anonymous. It was from an old friend of mine. He's secretary of Mining and Gen-

213

eral Metal Workers. Bill Hancock. He told me he was retiring this autumn. What he said was 'Come back here, and the job's yours. You've got a lot of friends up here. People who don't believe lies just because they're printed in newspapers. Politics is a dirty game. It's not your cup of tea. Come back home.' That seemed like sound advice to me, Prime Minister."

On the Friday morning Jonas returned to London. When he appeared in Lambard's office, Edward Lambard had to look twice to recognize him. His skin, which was normally pale, had reacted remarkably to a week of open air and blazing sun and was now a dark reddish brown. A handsome pair of mutton-chop whiskers had changed and broadened the outlines of his face. But it was not only his appearance. His personality seemed to have undergone a perceptible change. The most immediate impression was one of relaxation.

"There are one or two things I want to talk about," he said. "My mother died yesterday."

Lambard had noticed the black band on his arm. He said, "I'm very sorry."

"It wasn't unexpected," said Jonas. The tone in which he said it defied Lambard to be sympathetic. "I should be obliged if your firm would undertake the winding up of her estate. You acted for my father in his litigation against the North West Marine people. I believe it was your late senior partner, Arthur Sexton, who handled the compensation money he got from them."

"I was in the army at the time," said Lambard. "I don't remember the details, but we can get the files up easily enough. Did your mother leave a will?"

"I have it here. It's very short. She left everything to me. It's quite a substantial fund, and well invested. That's the next thing I wanted to talk about. I shall need four thousand pounds almost at once. I expect you can arrange a bridging loan from the bank?"

"That shouldn't be too difficult. But I don't suppose the appeal's going to cost anything like that."

"It's not the appeal. I'm buying a small general store and post office in a village called Sambourne, in Wiltshire. I've arranged with a local firm to handle the actual conveyancing. I shall move in as soon as it's completed."

"Move in?"

"Certainly."

"To run the shop?"

"Such is my intention. I think it has distinct possibilities. I plan to enlarge the scope of the business considerably. There are no real shopping centers nearer than Devizes on one side and Salisbury on the other. I see no reason why it should not develop other lines. Greengrocery, for instance. There are a lot of vegetables grown locally—they only want an outlet. Ironmongery too. There are endless possibilities."

"And your practice at Wimbledon?"

"I shall close it down. Now, if there is nothing else . . . I know you're a very busy man."

"Don't you want to hear about what happened on Monday and Tuesday?"

"Oh, the appeal. Yes. I read the report in the *Times*. I thought Cairns handled it very well."

"The general view is that we've got rather better than an even chance of success. You realize that if we get our order, there'll be a great deal to do."

"Yes," said Jonas. "That was something I did mean to mention." For the first time a very slight note of embarrassment had crept into his voice. "The fact is, I've decided not to take the matter any further."

Lambard stared at him, his mouth half open. He sometimes thought that thirty years in the law had deprived him of the faculty of surprise. He discovered that he was wrong. Before he could frame any adequate comment, Jonas had continued.

"As I see it, there's really no point in taking it any further. If we fail in the High Court, we can't proceed anyway. But we have at least demonstrated, I fancy, that there was a case to answer. If we win, we've demonstrated the point even more conclusively. There's nothing to be gained from rubbing it in. That would simply be vindictive. At least that's how I see it."

Lambard had recovered his voice. He said, "If the court gives you the order, surely you're obliged to pursue it."

"Certainly not," said Jonas sharply. "If I decide to drop the matter, no one can force me to take any step at all. The authorities could, of course, pursue the action themselves, if they wished to, but I don't see them doing it, do you?"

"No," said Lambard.

"That's how I reasoned it out. And that's the decision I came to."

"I suppose you realize that you've done Dylan almost irreparable harm."

"It was entirely his fault. If he'd admitted in the beginning that I was right, none of this would have happened, would it?"

"I suppose not," said Lambard.

Much of what happened afterward is a matter of recent history.

On July thirty-first, the last day of the legal term, the Court of Appeal rejected Jonas' application for an order of mandamus by two votes to one. Leave to appeal to the House of Lords was refused. This loosed a further storm of abuse from the press, but it had little to feed on, as neither of the principal characters in the drama seemed anxious to comment.

Will Dylan disappeared from the London scene with his family and buried himself in union affairs. Nobody imagined that this meant they had heard the last of him. When he does choose to reemerge into the public eye, Patrick may be able to use the profile which he completed with such pains and which hasn't yet been published.

When Christopher Martingale got back from his annual leave in August, Laurence Fairbrass offered him the job of taking charge of Jonas' abandoned practice. A solicitor can't just shut up shop like a greengrocer. There are too many things going on. Not only litigation. Trusts and administrations and half-finished conveyancing matters. The Law Society has to step in sometimes and help to clear up the mess.

Mutt advised him to take it. She never had a high opinion of him as an administrator. The Wimbledon office was a pretty fair shambles, but Willoughby agreed to stay on, and they gradually got things under control. Jonas wasn't much help. He was far too busy reorganizing the Sambourne General Stores.

The General Election was held in the second week of October. The government was thrown out and the Opposition came in with a majority of twenty-five seats. One of the first actions of the new government was to set up an official inquiry into the security services. Most of its hearings had to be *in camera*, and its report was a model of discretion.

Air Vice-Marshal Pulleyne was made a principal scapegoat and was removed from his job. But since no one felt able to explain what that job was, the effect of his dismissal was muted. Benz-Fisher was felt to be too dangerous to pursue, and his name was never mentioned publicly at all. He continued to live very happily with his blond girl friend in the hills above Grasse, drawing from time to time on one of his bank accounts in Switzerland.

One odd result of the election was that the new government honored, as it often does, the less controversial sections of the dissolution list of its predecessor, and Edward Lambard got his knighthood. As far as he was concerned, it was from the wrong party, but a detail like that didn't worry his wife.

Only the other day Jonas' name reappeared in the papers. It was a small paragraph in the *Evening Standard*, under the by-line "A Village Hampden." It reported that Jonas Killey, an ex-solicitor now running the village store and post office, was commencing proceedings against the local squire, Edwin Lamplough, to have a right of way across the park reopened.

Will Dylan read it. He felt deeply sorry for Mr. Lamplough.

218

406691

GILBERT
FLASH POINT
6.95

FEB - 3 1993
MAR 2 3 1994
SEP - 9 1997